A CARING HEART

Margaret Carr

CHIVERS

British Library Cataloguing in Publication Data available

This Large Print edition published by AudioGo Ltd, Bath, 2011
Published by arrangement with the Author

U.K. Hardcover ISBN 978 1 445 83678 2
U.K. Softcover ISBN 978 1 445 83679 9

Printed and bound in Great Britain by
MPG Books Group Limited

ISOBEL DISCOVERS THE CASUALTIES OF WAR

Winter clouds lay low among the high hills of North Northumberland as District Nurse, Isobel Ross, cycled up the muddy track towards Pine Tree Farm. The farm lay grey and square against the hillside like a piece of geology from another time.

Below her the road wound along the valley bottom for three miles until it came to the village of Thornbury, while above and around her the hills towered, and enclosed, their tops still capped in snow.

She arrived puffing and panting at the farm gate and dismounting propped her bicycle alongside the wall. A gaggle of geese came running towards her across the yard.

'Mrs Lewis,' she called, trying to make her voice heard above the noise of the geese. 'Mrs Lewis, it's Nurse Ross.'

After several minutes a small, grey-haired woman came out of the kitchen doorway and, picking up a broom, shooed away the geese—allowing Isobel to slip through the gate. Keeping on the right side of her rescuer Isobel edged her way to the safety of the house. Once inside she assumed her professional role and crossed to the man sitting waiting in the chair by the table.

1

of the window for hours at a time. He won't walk in the grounds with us or anything and he's as thin as a stick. I'm so worried, I can't think what I'll do when he comes home.'

Isobel could see that the poor woman was beside herself and tried to be as cheering as possible. 'Didn't the hospital warn you to expect changes in him when he came home?'

'Well yes, they did say that men who had lost limbs and mobility could take a long time to recover and that they may develop a bitter or difficult behaviour pattern, but we knew our boy wasn't the sort to cause trouble. I never lost a night's sleep with him when he was a baby, not even when he was teething. And he never gave us a minute's worry as a lad. Not like some folks' families you hear about.'

'Would you like me to talk to your son when he comes home?'

The woman's face lit up with relief. 'Oh, Nurse would you? I'd be ever so grateful.'

'No problem, Mrs Lewis. Now I must fly, I'll see you on Friday.'

'Goodbye, Nurse.'

Isobel put her bag into the basket on the front of the bike and climbing on board propelled herself down the steep uneven track to the valley floor. The cold wind nipped her ears beneath her uniform cap and she practised taking one hand at a time off the handlebars to hug it under her armpit for warmth.

4

The Lewis's son was the last thing on her mind as she reached the cosy little cottage known as the Nurse's Home. She pushed her bike into the garden shed and crossing to the back door went to lift the latch only to have the door open of its own accord.

'Hello, who's there,' she called, entering the kitchen and dumping her bag onto the worktop. She picked up and cuddled the welcoming cat. 'Who have you let into our home, Mr Churchill,' she asked the round, bewhiskered face of the gold and brown striped cat.

She looked up at the sound of heavy footfalls and gaped at the uniformed figure in the hall doorway. 'Alan.' It came out in a breathless whisper. 'Oh Alan!' The cat was dropped as she ran into the arms of the waiting man. His arms came around her and he held her close. When at last he released her she stood back and let her eyes wander over him, assuring herself that he was unharmed.

'How long do we have?'

He shook his head. 'Twenty-four hours, I report back in the morning.' She beamed at him and slowly his mouth lifted in a smile. 'It's good to see you, sis.'

She put everything in her pantry into a slap up meal and brought out a bottle of home-made elderberry wine she had been saving for just such an occasion. They had only each other, their parents having died of cancer one after the other several years ago. Each parent had been an only child and they had never known their grandparents.

After the meal they sat by the fire and Isobel talked while Alan listened. It hadn't always been like that in the past. Alan had been the boisterous one, full of fun and mischief, you couldn't shut him up. Slowly he'd changed as one by one his friends had been lost in dogfights and bombing raids.

It was during a long silence that Isobel thought of the Lewis's son again. Had he, like Alan, seen too much and lost too many to ever be the same person he had been before. Would his parents, she wondered, ever truly be able to understand what had happened to him?

Alan had been taught to fly by their father who had been a pilot in the First World War. He had enlisted in the Royal Air Force prior to the outbreak of war and at the ripe old age of twenty-nine was already considered a veteran of many missions.

Clock chimes alerted her to the time. She was due at evening surgery in ten minutes. Alan assured her he was quite happy napping in the chair by the fire until her return.

*   *   *

The surgery was in the back room of the doctor's house. She made her way through the crowded waiting room acknowledging the nods and murmured greetings.

'Ah, Nurse there are two idiots in need of patching up after a brawl, perhaps you will attend to them.' Doctor Turnbull snapped on her entrance. He was a small wiry man with a brusque manner that put many people on their guard, but he was the only doctor for several miles and in Isobel's opinion a good one.

'Certainly, Doctor.' She called the men in one at a time and cleaned and sticky-plastered their wounds with the exception of a cut eyebrow that needed stitching and a head wound that needed pressure to stop it bleeding.

The last on the list was Bobby Dunn and Isobel sighed. Bobby lived in a shack on the moors. He was invariably drunk, dirty and lousy. He had been told time and again never to come to the surgery until the waiting room was empty to avoid contaminating everyone else.

The doctor turned his head and gave Isobel a sympathetic glance as Bobby ambled into the room. For every time the old man came it meant Isobel had to stay behind after surgery and disinfect the whole place.

'What's wrong with you, man,' the doctor growled.

'I need something for m' innards, m'guts is killing me.'

'The only thing killing you is the drink. I've

told you before cut the drinking; you'll get nothing from me until you do.'

The old man bent over the doctor's desk and cried, 'It's not the drink, I tell you. It's m'guts. I've been poisoned.' He shook his head.

Isobel could see the lice falling onto the desktop.

'Get across the room,' the doctor bellowed, wafting his desk top with some papers.

'Just give me something to help, Doc, and I'll go.'

Turning to Isobel, Doctor Turnbull said, 'Give him a bottle of SGM, Nurse, and get him out of here.'

As Isobel was wiping down ledges, the desk and chairs, the cleaner arrived. Isobel had to smile when the woman said, 'I see old Bobby's been here again, Nurse. He's a terrible disgrace that man. They should lock him up, he's a health hazard to decent people, he is.'

'It's the drink,' Isobel excused him.

'Drink be blowed. It's all that rummaging around in people's bins, why he leaves more mess behind him than the deer when they come down off the top, and it can't be good for him eating rubbish. Why just last night her that lives next to the church put some of that DDT around her bins to keep prowling animals away.'

Isobel was horrified. 'She shouldn't be doing that, anyone's cat or dog might pick it up.'

8

'Only strays, mind you.' The woman commented continuing with her mopping.

Isobel decided to keep Mr Churchill indoors until she could speak to the woman who so carelessly spread poison around her bins. She finished up what she was doing and left the surgery with a cheery, 'Goodnight,' to the cleaner.

As she walked back to the cottage however, her thoughts kept returning to the poison and just as she reached her door she knew why. Had Bobby taken something from the bins that had been contaminated with the poison? Much as she wanted to spend precious time with Alan, she knew she wouldn't rest until she had been up to the shack to check on him.

When she told Alan of her decision he insisted he accompany her. It was dark by now, so armed with two torches they set out along the main street of the village and up the back path to the moors and Bobby's home. The flame of an oil lamp flickered in the window as they approached the shack. A cold wind made Isobel shiver. There was no answer when Alan rapped on the door.

'We should just go in,' she said. 'The chances are that he's sleeping off the drink.'

So they opened the creaking door and went in. The air was heavy with the stench of sour drink and body odour. Alan shone his torch around revealing a table littered with empty cans and dirty food packets on which

9

cockroaches were feasting.

'Stay there,' Alan ordered his sister, as he moved forward to investigate a second room. Moving forward with care he prodded the body on the bed. Bobby groaned.

Outside for a breath of clean air, Alan told Isobel that the man was still alive but had been sick.

'If there is any chance at all that he has accidentally taken that poison then we must get him to hospital,' she said. 'You will have to go back down to the village and phone for an ambulance.'

'Is there no-one in the village who could take him to the hospital?'

'Not in his state, no.'

'I don't like leaving you here on your own.'

Isobel gave a gentle smile. 'I'm in no danger, not like you are every time you fly out on a mission.'

He gave her shoulder a quick squeeze then turned and headed off down the path back to the village. It was half-an-hour before he returned to tell her that an ambulance was on its way, and a further hour before two men arrived panting up the hill to the shack. One of the men carried a rolled up stretcher and Isobel led them inside.

When they came out carrying an unconscious Bobby between them, after letting Isobel know what they thought of the conditions they had found him in, they asked

Alan to light their way back down the path to the ambulance. 'I have to go with him,' she told Alan regretfully as they stood and watched the men loading the stretcher into the ambulance.

'How will you get back?'

She shrugged, 'I'll get a lift back.'

'I'll be here until noon.'

Isobel could feel the familiar lump in her throat as she wrapped her arms around his neck. 'I'll be back before you go,' she promised. Then she climbed into the waiting ambulance and the doors slammed shut.

*   *   *

Friday morning saw Isobel back at the gate of Pine Tree Farm waiting for her escort across the yard. Some unseen event had upset the geese that morning for they came charging at the gate heads extended, hissing and jabbing at the rails. Terrified of the creatures, Isobel, after a swift look round to make sure no one was watching, lashed out with her bag at the two heads stuck through the gate. The heads were withdrawn but her swipe at them seemed to have infuriated them more and even Mrs Lewis when she arrived had trouble chasing them off.

'How are you this morning, Duncan?' Isobel asked upon entering the kitchen.

'Just the same, Nurse,' he said, pulling up

his trouser leg. 'The wife says you'll be talking to our Jack when you've finished with my leg.'

Isobel looked up from washing her hands. 'He's home?'

'Yes,' he looked over her head to where his wife stood beside the sink. 'Thing is, it isn't easy, Nurse,' and here he took a deep sigh.

'No of course it won't be easy at first, but things will settle down.'

'I don't mean . . . thing is he wants to die, and he's asked me to help him.'

Isobel halted in the middle of treating his leg and gazed up at the man's face, set now in grim lines. Her heart jumped a beat then, settled down again. 'He'll be depressed, Duncan, he won't know what he's saying.'

She heard Mrs Lewis's quiet sobs behind her. Swiftly finishing off her work on the ulcer she stood up and crossing to the sink, washed her hands once more. Drying them on the towel she said, 'Right, I'll see him now if you will be so kind as to lead the way, Mrs Lewis.'

They left the kitchen and walked down an inside passage to the door of the front room. Opening the door and stepping softly inside Mrs Lewis said in a quiet voice, 'There's someone to see you, Jack. It's Nurse Ross.'

A chair was set in front of a tall window and all Isobel could see of the occupier was the back of his dark head. She nodded to Mrs Lewis indicating that the woman could go now. Then she walked across the room until she was

12

standing alongside the chair. There was a beautiful view through the window of a river winding its way through the surrounding hills, like a silver ribbon wrapping an untidy parcel. For a while there was silence. Then Isobel said, 'My brother is a fighter pilot.'

The man in the chair nodded his head in recognition of her statement. When she looked down at him she knew his mother was right to worry. The skin on his face was parchment thin and stretched over sharp bones. Deep blue eyes were sunk back and stared from dark caverns with a fixed gaze. His clothes hung from his collarbones like washing on a line and thick black hair lay limp and greasy on his skull.

'Do you like what you see?' The voice was strong but weary.

'It's a beautiful view,' she said, deliberately misunderstanding him. He must have been a good looking man once, she thought. Now most of his cheek and lower jaw had been remodelled and looked tight and raw. She gazed out through the window again before asking suddenly, 'Do you like the countryside?'

'I did, once,' he said, with bitterness.

'I do a lot of walking in the hills. It gives you a great sense of perspective, I find.'

'Well, I won't be walking anywhere any more so is there some point to this visit?'

'Only to make you aware of how much your parents are hurting.'

'I am only too aware, thank you.'

What would I do if he were Alan, she wondered. Alan had changed, she recognised that, but even so he was a fighter. In this man's place he would fight back she was sure of it.

'Your life is precious to them if not to yourself. They're lost; they don't know how to help you. They need you and if you can see that you may also see a way forward for yourself. Please try.'

Silence was the only answer and eventually she turned and left.

* * *

'Does your son have any friends locally?' she asked his mother on her way out.

'He's always been a quiet boy, didn't make many friends, but the ones he did make stayed.'

'And have any of these friends been to see him?'

She looked shocked. 'Oh no, he wouldn't let us tell anyone what had happened.'

'I see. Well thank you for this little chat, but I must get on.' She laid a hand on the older woman's arm. 'Jack's recovery will take a long time, Mrs Lewis but he'll improve, I'm sure of it.'

'Thank you, Nurse.'

* * *

14

At morning surgery the following Monday she asked Doctor Turnbull if she could have a word. She brought him up to date on Duncan Lewis's ulcer then went on to mention Jack.

He hummed and hawed for a while then he looked over the top of his glasses and asked, 'You're going to take up this psychiatric clap trap, are you, Nurse?'

'Of course not, Doctor.'

'Glad to hear it. You don't need me to tell you that men are being shot at and blown up every day. Unfortunately it's what war is all about. Frequently they are patched up and sent out again unless they end up like this lad in which case there is nothing to be done but learn to live with it. It's no good reminding him that he should be glad to be alive when so many of his friends are not.'

'But he wants to die and has asked his father to help him.'

'Then it's to be hoped his father has more sense. Time, that's the great healer, give him time to adapt.'

For once she disagreed with the doctor's summation of the situation. In this case she felt sure that time would only worsen Jack Lewis's depression.

On her next visit to the farm the track up from the road was near impassable. It had rained all night and the unsurfaced track was like a waterfall. She had been soaked twice on

15

her morning rounds and dried off each time by the kindness of her patients' families. Now, as she skittered and slithered her way up the track getting soaked through once more, she finally gave up riding and dismounting from the bike continued to push it against the roaring water.

Not caring where the geese were she let herself in through the gate and across the yard to the back door of the farmhouse. Mrs Lewis frowned as she greeted her.

'Oh dear, Nurse. You shouldn't have come up here today.'

Isobel smiled. 'I had other patients to see Mrs Lewis, but I must admit I wouldn't have minded borrowing the doctor's car just for today.'

'Duncan's bringing the sheep down for the lambing. If you take your coat off I'll put it in front of the range here to dry.'

'Thank you. How is Jack?'

'Just the same, he's eaten hardly anything, though I've made him all his old favourite things, game pie, suet pudding, and one of my bran cakes. He used to love a bit of that with a piece of cheese.' Her eyes began to fill and she turned away.

Isobel shook off her uniform coat and hat, rubbed her short blonde hair with the towel the woman had given her and sighed. 'Well why don't I pop in and see him while I wait for Duncan.'

16

'You know where he is.'

Isobel nodded and headed down the passage to the front room. She tapped on the door and walked in.

'What do you want?'

'Just a chat, I'm waiting for your father. He has a nasty ulcer that needs attending to.'

'So I believe, and if I was any use at all I would be out there helping him.'

'So why aren't you?'

He turned towards her and lifting his mouth on the good side of his face, gave a half smile. 'What do you suggest I would be good for? I could hammer in a fence post with my false leg I suppose,' he said, rapping the said leg with the walking stick he kept near to hand. 'Or perhaps I could just sit there and count sheep.'

Isobel sat herself on the end of the bed and faced him across the room. 'Well self pity won't help him, and you are right he does need help.'

Just for a moment the bleakness in his gaze frightened her, and then he flung his stick across the room and turned his back on her.

'OK, so you need to get your strength back first.' She spoke quietly. 'Does the leg still bother you?' All she got was a grunt in response, but the lift of his chin told her that it did. 'You need to eat, little and often and exercise. I'll speak to your mother and see that she doesn't overdo your meals, if you promise to exercise more.'

17

Getting up from the bed she walked over to where the stick lay on the floor and picking it up took it back to him. He accepted it without a word then turned to stare out of the window.

Duncan was home when she returned to the kitchen and both parents turned towards her as she entered the room. 'A little homemade broth or a coddled egg, small light meals little and often, Mrs Lewis. Leave the suet dumplings and pies until he's a bit stronger.'

Then turning back to Duncan she said, ushering him into the chair, 'If you could just find something he could do to help out on the farm, it might stop him brooding about himself.'

'There'll be plenty to do when the lambing starts, but I don't want to pressure the lad.'

'I don't think he's about to let you pressurise him into anything, but he needs to be active. So anything you can get him to do will help. And see if you can't have a word with one or two of those friends of his to let them know he is home. You don't have to ask them around just make them aware of the situation and leave it up to them.'

'Right-oh, Nurse,' he said, as Isobel got to work on his leg.

Her damp coat lay heavy on her shoulders as she said her goodbyes and headed off down the slippery track back to the road and the village.

AN ACCIDENT ON THE FARM

Jack knew he was being unfair to his parents but he couldn't help himself. He raged inwardly at the injustices in life. Why must the Almighty take his leg, when it left him so useless that he might as well be dead?

His mother knocked on the door and came into the room carrying a bowl of soup and a cup of tea. She placed them on the small table by the bed and gave him one of her gentle smiles that made his eyes glaze with unshed tears. It was all he could do to turn his back and stare out of the window.

At least in the hospital he had been one of many, his nightmares subdued by tablets. Here at home he was afraid to sleep for fear of screaming. What little memory he had of that fatal return journey, after being hit from ground fire and losing an engine, he had tried to bury in the reality of his fight to keep the old girl aloft. His co-pilot was dead, his crew depending on him alone to get them home.

Moving over to the table he ate the soup and drank the tea.

When he closed his eyes he was back there under the stars, smarting air from a hole in the window cooling his over-heated face. Voices in his head urging him onward. His journey was timeless for he never landed. Waking up to the reality of life was when the screaming began. Never being sure of whether awake or asleep the crying was a hellish nightmare filled with the urgency and fear of what awaited him.

It was morning when his father came to ask if he would lead the horse in after Duncan and the old shepherd, Ned Craig, had unloaded some feed for the sheep. 'I'd have brought him back myself but Ned wants me to give him a hand over the top and the lad isn't here yet.'

Jack turned from the window where he had been watching the sun breaking through what had promised to be a miserable day. He wasn't sure how he felt. He hadn't left the room since his arrival. Now here was his dad asking him for help. He found himself nodding and reaching for his jacket. Slowly he followed his father from the room.

*   *   *

Bobby Dunn was back on the moor, the local policeman, Constable Burns told Isobel some days later. 'He walked out of the hospital without as much as a bye your leave, Nurse. How he got back here heaven alone knows, but back he is, he was seen not half-an-hour ago by the postie.'

'Oh no, that place of his isn't fit for pigs let alone a sick man.'

'I'll be having a word with him, but I can't force him to go back to the hospital if he doesn't want to.'

'Well somebody will have to do something about that shack, who does it belong to?'

'I'll be making enquiries.'

The news spread around the village so fast that when Isobel entered the surgery that morning Doctor Turnbull announced stiffly that Bobby Dunn couldn't have been that ill when he was back so soon. Isobel knew he was in a grouch because he had failed to give Bobby the benefit of the doubt when the man had complained of a bad stomach.

*　　　*　　　*

That afternoon, while she was making herself a cup of tea, a crash and a thud had her hurrying through to her front room where a rock lay on her living room floor with broken glass all around it. 'What on earth,' she gasped. Figures flashed past her window to the clatter of passing feet and dissenting voices.

Isobel rushed to her front door and flinging it open stepped out into the garden. The street was remarkable empty for five-fifteen on a midweek afternoon.

Kids, she thought angrily, stepping back inside to survey the damage. She removed the stone and swept up the glass before going off to find something to cover the hole with until she could persuade Macky, the local odd job man to replace the window.

Later, as she passed the Anderson shelters in the allotments on her way to evening surgery she noticed children playing and it struck her then that the shadows passing her window at the time of the rock incident had been rather too large to have been children. It was just a passing thought and was gone by the time she entered a near empty waiting room.

'Where is everyone?' she asked Doctor Turnbull.

The doctor was scribbling away at his desk and didn't raise his head as he said, 'Be thankful for small mercies, Nurse.'

'Yes, Doctor.'

Darkness had fallen by the time she hurried along to the little shop on the corner of the street. The Mackenzies lived above the shop and while his wife ran the business, Macky worked when he felt like it, with odd jobs here and there. His great excuse was the part he played in the Home Guard, though no bombs or Germans had made there way to Thornbury as yet.

The shop was shut and Isobel was on the point of rattling on the street door when who should come along the street but Macky and some of his Home Guard friends. About to open her mouth, Macky called to her from down the road.

'Ah, Nurse. Just the person we were looking for. Sorry about the window, it was an accident. I'll be up in the morning to fix it.'

22

The other men with him were nodding their heads in agreement.

Isobel could hardly believe her ears. 'Accident? You mean you threw that rock through my window? Why on earth would you do such a thing?'

'It wasn't meant see,' one of the others piped up. 'We were chasing that dolt, Bobby Dunn.'

Isobel stared at them through the dusk. 'You were what?'

'He's back in the village, Nurse, and the wives are going mad they don't want him back here, he's always hanging around the school kitchens and folks' bins. And that filthy old coat he wears could stand up by itself.'

A tall man at the back said, 'Kids are always hanging around him teasing him with one thing or another, so when our Sam got the nits it didn't take any guessing to know where they had come from.'

'That's rubbish, anyone can get hair lice,' Isobel said, feeling her skin begin to crawl at the very thought of them. 'Bobby is not a well man, for you to be hounding him is cruel. I have already asked Constable Burns to look into the matter, so any more rocks flying around and he will know where to come.' Turning her back on them she stomped off down the road.

*   *   *

The next day Isobel was cycling out of the village on her rounds. As she reached the turn off for the farm she saw Duncan and his horse and cart approaching from the opposite direction. When it drew near she saw it was Jack not Duncan in the driving seat. He stopped and scowling down at her said, 'Throw your machine on and climb aboard, I'll give you a lift up.'

'Thanks,' she called, lifting the bike onto the back of the open cart and jumping up behind it. 'I'm pleased to see you're out and about,' she shouted, straightening her cap and jiggling around to make herself more comfortable as the cart bounced and jerked over the humps and hollows of the track.

Soon they made their way into the safety of the farmyard, only to be surrounded by geese. Isobel was contemplating throwing the bike at them and making a run for the kitchen doorway when Jack came around and lifting down her bicycle stood waiting for her to drop to the ground.

Gingerly she let herself slide slowly to the ground watching warily for any threatened attack on her ankles. She took the handlebars from a grim faced Jack and edged slowly away from him. The geese had been known to attack the tyres of her bicycle on occasion which was why she now usually left it outside the gate. A sudden noise behind her had the

24

geese scattering with fluttering wings and angry cries and Isobel bolted for the safety of the farmhouse.

'You did that deliberately,' she accused Jack as he entered the kitchen a short while later.

She was just finishing off bandaging Duncan's leg. Duncan looked up surprised. 'Who did what deliberately?'

Mrs Lewis coming in from the passage smiled. 'Nurse Ross is afraid of the geese and Jack chased them.'

Duncan cocked an eyebrow at Isobel as Jack limped over to the sink to wash his hands. Isobel rose from her task and stood alongside him waiting her turn. His mother handed him a towel. He has the hands of an artist Isobel thought, as she watched him shake the water from his long fingers and take the towel.

When he was finished he handed the towel to her and her heart did a tumble at the simple intimacy of the gesture. Though he was still terribly thin his mother assured her he was eating better.

'Just like you said, Nurse, little and often,' she said after the inner door had closed behind him.

'He'll be all right now,' Duncan said. 'He wasn't too happy the first time I asked him to give me a hand, but as long as I don't make too much of it he's OK.'

Isobel's twice-weekly visits to Pine Tree Farm were on Tuesdays and Fridays and

25

followed by a call on Mrs Foster, a worker at Hill Farm, on the opposite side of the valley. The ride up was winding but not as steep as the Pine Tree Road, and much smoother.

The maternity case was not going well. The widow had been allowed to keep her tied cottage on account that she worked the land. Today when Isobel arrived the pregnant woman was feeding the cows in the byre. Her youngest sat in a nearby manger while the other two played in the straw on the floor.

'How are you, Mrs Foster?'

'Tired, Nurse,' she said, stopping what she was doing and leaning on the pitchfork.

'I thought the doctor warned you the last time.'

'I know, Nurse. I've always fallen quick. My hubby used to say he couldn't hang his trousers on the bedpost afore I'd be off again.' She was a tall middle-aged woman with badly swollen legs and red hair tied back with binder twine. 'I'm right glad Farmer Heron sent word to Doctor Turnbull mind. He's right good to work for, Farmer Heron. Many would have sent me and the kids packing when my man died a couple of months back, but he let me stay on. I'm a good worker though, if I say it myself and I have a good neighbour who doesn't mind helping me with the kiddies.'

'Are you eating properly?' Isobel asked, keeping one eye on the precariously seated youngster in the manger who was chewing hard on the dolly peg in its fists.

'I'm fine, Nurse. They killed a pig next door a while since and let me have a piece, a good bit of belly pork and tatties and you can't go far wrong.' She gave a hearty laugh. 'I'm afraid I can't offer you a cup of tea cos we're right out at the moment on account of the rationing.'

'That's all right, Mrs Foster. I'll let you get on with your work.'

As Isobel cycled away she was far from happy at the situation, but there was little she could do about it other than to keep an eye on how the woman coped.

Two more visits then she would be finished for the weekend and if she was lucky there may be some communication from Alan.

Originally he had been stationed down south but six months ago he had been brought up north and now was stationed somewhere in Yorkshire, so she was hopeful of seeing more of him.

Churchill was in the sulks and although he came forward to greet her on her return he refused to be cuddled. This was all because he had been kept indoors until the woman who lived next door to the church had swept up the poison and promised Constable Burns she would refrain from laying down poison again. The constable had made enquires about Bobby's shack from the landowners and discovered that it had at one time been used as

27

a keeper's cottage. However, when the new cottage was built the old one had been forgotten, which was when Bobby had moved in.

Some days after the incident of the stone through her window, Isobel heard that the shack had been burnt to the ground. Who was responsible she never discovered but it meant that Bobby was taken into the workhouse. Macky had replaced the glass in her window and she was looking forward to a peaceful weekend.

Sunday morning arrived chilly but bright and Isobel, disappointed at not having had word of Alan, decided to go for a walk. She would have liked to own a dog. Mr Churchill was a wonderful pet but more like a pair of comfy slippers rather than a walking companion. She made her way up onto the moors where the air was fresh and clear. The wind tugged her hair and the pewits dived and called their shrill cry. Rabbits scampered around a grassy hillock riddled with warrens.

As she moved on up the hill and into the shaded cover of pine trees she watched a herd of deer crossing the path above her. The movement of birds and small mammals crackled in the undergrowth around her and the tops of the trees whispered in the wind overhead.

A bare piece of ground to her right was bathed in light and as she glanced at the wonderful picture it made with shafts of sunlight slanting through the branches, a shadow moved across the space.

Coming to a halt, she frowned, wondering if her eyes had deceived her. Another walker perhaps, but for some reason she didn't think so. Curious, she moved forward. Now she could see other things in the clearing, a rough shelter, a dead fire, a line of what looked like a variety of bottles and jars. Could it be a hide for someone watching wildlife? No, they would hardly be likely to have a fire if that was the case.

Then she saw him and could hardly believe her eyes. He looked up at the same time and saw her. He stood staring at her without saying a word. 'Bobby, what on earth are you doing up here?'

'They burnt it,' he shouted at her. 'They burnt m'house.'

She walked into the clearing and looked about her. 'But you can't live here. I thought you were in the workhouse in Rennington.'

He shook his great bear-like head. 'Bad place. They burnt it.'

'Why was the workhouse a bad place, Bobby? They would have fed you, and given you a place to sleep?'

'Bad people,' he turned away from her and began to wander off into the forest.

Made him bathe and clean himself up no doubt, Isobel thought. But what was he

29

surviving on and there was no drink available here. She went to follow him but he turned and shouted at her to go away. So she fell back to the clearing and decided to wait.

Sitting on a tree stump she thought to give him half-an-hour then she would have to return home. She should inform the police of his presence here in the woods but somehow she felt reluctant to do that. She worried as to how he would survive. The lack of bathing and laundry wouldn't bother him but without any social influence of any kind wouldn't he revert to an animal-like existence, and she couldn't let that happen.

On the point of leaving she heard him returning and watched in amazement as he entered the clearing and dropped two rabbits and two fish down by the fire. 'Traps,' he said, nodding his head, and taking a knife from his pocket started to clean them.

Isobel watched in fascination as he skinned and cleaned the rabbits then covered them in mud which he made from the water in one of his jars. Now he stirred the ashes of the seemingly dead fire and placing the covered rabbits in a hollow covered them with ash before bringing the fire back to life again. Once small flames began to appear he gutted the fish and skewering a hole through them stuck them on a branch and rested them across the two hearthstones one on either side of the fire.

Isobel sighed. In the short time she had been here in the clearing Bobby had provided himself with not only one meal but two. The variety of jars and bottles were his water supply obviously from some source nearby. Satisfied that she no longer needed to worry about his welfare, other than his lack of company, she said goodbye to him and returned to the village.

*   *   *

When next she visited the Lewises there was no reply to her call for Mrs Lewis to come to her aid with the broom. So she was left with no option but to cross the yard taking her bike with her and keeping it between her and the geese.

The kitchen door opened to the lift of the latch, but the kitchen when she entered it was empty. Calling still brought no response and with a puzzled frown she went through into the front room in search of Jack. Again the room was empty.

The open doors didn't surprise her for country folk rarely locked their doors. But to find the place totally deserted when they knew she would be visiting was a surprise. Moving to the back door she looked out across the yard and up the hillside beyond. There was no sign of a living soul anywhere. She went back inside and made herself a cup of tea. Time passed and still they hadn't returned. Worried now she knew she would have to leave if she was to cover her other calls. So she scribbled a short message and leaving it on the table left the house.

She called at the doctor's first thing next morning to inform him that she would be fitting a second visit to the Lewis's into her schedule, and was shocked when he said, 'No need, Duncan Lewis was injured yesterday and is in the Royal Hospital.'

'Why, what happened?'

The doctor looked at her over the top of his glasses. 'He fell and hit his head. He has yet to recover consciousness.'

Isobel bit back her concern knowing full well that the doctor would think it very unprofessional of her to show any personal feelings. 'Have we any idea how long he will be in hospital?'

'None at all, it depends entirely when, and if, he recovers consciousness.'

'I'll cross them off my list then until I hear otherwise.'

'That will be for the best. How is Mrs Foster coming along?'

'She has oedema and her blood pressure is a little high, but apart from that she seems to be managing as well as can be expected in the circumstances.'

He continued down the list of Isobel's patients asking after each and every one of them. And this was what endeared him to Isobel, for no matter how rude or gruff and outspoken he was she knew that deep down he cared deeply about the health and well-being of each and every one of them.

'Have you had any word from your brother?'

'No, Doctor.'

'Ah well he'll be busy keeping those Germans off our backs, no doubt. He'll be home soon I'm sure.'

A few days later Isobel decided to make an unofficial call on the Lewis's. She had heard some unpleasant rumours in the village hinting that Jack had been responsible for his father's fall.

Mrs Lewis came out at her call. 'What can I do for you, Nurse? Duncan's not here,' she told Isobel, as she came up to the gate.

'I know that, Mrs Lewis. This is just a social visit to make sure you're all right, and to ask if there is anything I can do to help.'

'Thank you, Nurse, but the doctor's told me there is nothing anyone can do until Duncan wakes up, but if you'd like to come in for a cup of tea I wouldn't mind the company.' For once the geese ignored them as they crossed the yard to the kitchen.

Once inside Joyce Lewis made the tea and they both sat down in front of the fire range surrounded by a crate and a couple of cardboard boxes in which lay five sleeping lambs.

'They'll wake up soon enough and then we won't be able to make ourselves heard above the noise,' Joyce Lewis said. 'I don't know what we will do without Duncan. Old Ned is a grand help, but he's getting on in years and young Billy Mackenzie who helps out part time, can't wait for his call up papers to come through. The neighbours are all lending a hand with the lambing but . . .' Her normally worried expression was more deeply etched than usual and she made no attempt to drink her tea.

'What about Jack?'

The woman's chin wobbled and the cup rattled in its saucer. 'In his room. He blames himself for Duncan's accident but it wasn't his fault.'

'What happened?' Isobel asked, gently taking the cup and saucer from the woman's hand.

Mrs Lewis sniffed then pulling herself together she said, 'Duncan was in the barn sorting through some gates for the sheep pens. He had climbed over a pile of other stuff and when he found what he wanted he turned to hand them to Jack, but Jack couldn't reach them and Duncan slipped and fell.' She hesitated and gulped a mouth full of air before carrying on. 'He hit his head on the concrete floor. Jack was standing over him when I went out to call them in for dinner. We don't know

34

how long he had been there because Jack couldn't tell us.

'A neighbour called the ambulance and I went to the hospital with Duncan. I came home this morning on the bus because I couldn't leave the farm and Jack for long. They promised they would send word the minute Duncan wakes,' she said, raising her face to Isobel as though seeking confirmation.

'Of course they will. They will probably telephone Constable Burns who will come up and tell you what is happening.'

'I was hoping Jack . . . but he won't answer the door. He was in his room when I got home and he hasn't come out since.'

'Let me try,' Isobel said, getting to her feet.

She went down the passage and knocked on the door of the front room. 'Jack, it's Nurse Isobel. Please let me in, I have to talk to you.'

Silence.

'It's news from the hospital, about your father,' she lied.

With her ear pressed to the door she could hear movement, so she stood back and waited but still nothing happened.

'Jack if you don't or can't answer I shall have to call on Doctor Turnbull who will probably send for help and you will be taken back to hospital.'

There was a scuffle then the door was slowly cracked open. Dark eyes flashed in a white stubbled face. 'Go away,' he snarled.

35

She could smell the stuffy air of neglect in the room. 'No, stop being so self-pitying and come and help your mother.'

'What news from the hospital?'

'The local policeman is going to bring a message when your father wakes up.' He went to slam the door, but with the speed of a lamb at an open gate she shot her foot in the doorway.

'Come on, let me in, we have to talk.'

'Say what you have to say then get out,' he snarled.

Isobel sat on the end of the unmade bed and stared at the back of his head. Speaking quietly she asked, 'Where did it happen?'

'In the barn. I couldn't move, he just lay there and I couldn't move.'

'So you froze, it happens. But he's in hospital now and being well looked after. Your mother needs your support now.'

'I couldn't help my father though could I!' he cried. 'Your time's up. Get out.'

The anguish in his voice made her long to comfort him, but she rose to her feet and left him, shutting the door softly behind her.

'WHAT ARE YOU DOING HERE?'

It was nearly a week before she called again at the farm. Duncan Lewis was still in a coma.

Mrs Lewis came hurrying from the dairy as Isobel arrived. 'Is there any news of Duncan, Nurse?'

'No, I'm sorry if you thought I was bringing a message. I was just calling to check on Jack.'

Her face lost what little colour it had as she put down her pail. 'He went back to the hospital the day before yesterday. Walked down to the village and caught the bus into Rennington. Just said, "It's better I go, Mam," and off he went.'

'Did he say why?'

'No, he just walked away. He'd been very quiet since your last visit and had come out of his room and started to eat again. But he was no help on the farm. I had hoped, but it wasn't to be.' She sighed.

Isobel felt her spirits sink as she turned her bike back down the hill. Guilt swamped her, she had thought to help but it appeared she had said the wrong thing.

*   *   *

'No, Nurse you mustn't think that. If the boy has gone back to the hospital voluntarily it's because he knows he needs further treatment. He will be well looked after there, they are dealing with the war wounded all the time,' Doctor Turnbull assured her later that day.

'I just hope I said nothing to make him think he had to go back.'

'I'm sure you didn't, now can we get back to business. I have a telephone message here from the authorities at the workhouse. Apparently Bobby Dunn was supposed to be admitted and they are asking if we have him.' He looked up over his glasses and scowled at her. 'What in the name of all that's holy do they think we are running here, a missing persons' bureau? Have you seen the wretched man about, Nurse?'

Isobel was standing with her back to him when she answered. 'No, Doctor, I'm afraid I haven't seen him in the village at all.'

'Umm, probably moved on,' he said, pushing the message to one side.

Isobel wondered about Bobby. It had rained last night and she doubted that his shelter was weather-proof. The workhouse wouldn't have bothered to ring unless they had some idea that he might be in trouble. They didn't like the police to get in first and show them up in a bad light. But Isobel knew the only danger Bobby might be to the general public was as a health hazard.

The following afternoon she decided to go back to Bobby's den. She would take Alan's old camping gear he'd had since his Boy Scout days and a share of her precious provisions. After packing everything carefully into the kit bag she rolled up the rubber groundsheet and tied it firmly at one end then playing out the cord, tied it around the other end leaving a

38

length of cord to sling around her shoulders.

Not wanting to be seen by anyone on the front street, she left by the back door and down through the garden to the back lane. From here she would join the path up onto the moors a little higher than at the bottom of the main road out of the village.

She passed two boys with worms arguing as to which one was the longest and not long after that a gypsy woman gathering herbs. The path was muddy in places and twice she nearly slipped.

Once into the woods however, the going was easier and it wasn't long before she came to the clearing where Bobby was living.

A large flat stone had been placed across the two side stones to protect the fire from the rain. Bobby was chopping wood and gathering and piling more brush against the sides of his shelter to give him extra cover. He stopped what he was doing when he saw her enter the clearing. He must have realised I might have informed the authorities of his whereabouts, she thought, yet he had made no effort to move on.

'I've brought you some things, Bobby.'

He grinned. 'Good things?' he asked, hovering around her like a child impatient for presents.

'I hope so,' she said, untying her bundles and laying them down at his feet. 'There's a ground sheet and some cocoa and dried milk

39

for a hot drink and a primus stove and matches incase your fire goes out. In here,' she said, pulling out the interlocked tins, 'are your billycan, a pan, plate and mug. In this bag is some bread and cheese, half a cornbeef pie and two apples.'

She pulled some cutlery out of one of her coat pockets and a bag of sweets out of the other. She had been keeping the Black Bullets for Alan, but at the last minute decided that her brother wouldn't mind sacrificing them and she handed them over to Bobby.

'Tools?' Bobby asked.

Isobel shook her head. 'I can't Bobby, I don't have any.'

'Need tools,' he repeated. Leaving the things she had brought him where they lay he turned and went back to his work stacking brush.

She watched him for a while as he worked. He seemed to know what he was about. The shelter was looking more solid already.

'Don't you miss other people,' she asked.

'People don't like me, I don't like people.'

'Some people like you,' she said, though right at that moment she couldn't bring a name to mind.

'No,' he said, shaking his great head as he put the last branch in place and stood back to admire his handywork.

'I haven't told anyone where you are but if you want anything, or are ill, you must come and find me. You know where I live, don't you, Bobby?'

He looked round at her and grinned. 'The Nurse's Home, you have a cat who likes chicken. I like chicken.'

She had a sudden horrified vision of Bobby raiding her bins for chicken bones, and pulling her coat more closely around her she made to leave.

As she headed back towards the track she told herself she was a fool for bothering about the old tramp, he seemed perfectly capable of fending for himself and it wasn't really her responsibility to inform the authorities on his whereabouts.

*　　　*　　　*

There was a letter from Alan in the post next morning. He was being moved up to an airfield in Scotland and would have a forty-eight hour pass which he would spend with her on his way up.

She read the newspapers and was well aware of the battle going on for Norway. What other reason could the Air Force have for sending him up into Scotland other than it being a jumping off place for Norway?

That evening she pooled all the rations she had and baked a vegetable pie, and a sponge cake without sugar. She was lucky enough to have eggs and bacon donated by her grateful patients and there was still half a cup of dripping in the larder.

Next she set about baking the rested bread she had set by the fire earlier. Sweat dribbled down her face and she raised a hand to wipe it away as she stood back to admire her handywork. It was near midnight by the time she had finished and she went to bed tired but well satisfied.

In the early hours she was woken by someone rattling on her door. Grumbling to herself she climbed out of bed and headed down the stairs, stopping only to pull on her dressing gown and shove her feet into slippers. Doctor Turnbull was standing on the doorstep.

'You sleep like the dead, woman. Get dressed, we are wanted up at Beacon Hill.'

He turned and stomped off back to the car. Isobel dashed upstairs to dress and was down again in minutes, grabbing her bag as she hurried out to the waiting car.

'Heron's wife has had a heart attack.' He was grinding the gears as the little Austin tore out of the village and along the valley road. It was still dark as they turned up into the hills. It had begun to rain and the wipers creaked as they half-heartedly swiped across the window. He grumbled low in his chest as the headlights picked out three deer lying under the moorland bankside. They got slowly to their feet seemingly reluctant to move over, as he pushed along the narrow road.

They reached the farm and were shown straight upstairs. Hazel Heron lay with her eyes closed against a mound of pillows. Her breathing was shallow and erratic. The farmer sat by the bed holding his wife's hand.

'Good to see you, Turnbull,' he said rising to his feet and taking the doctor's hand in a firm grip. 'It came on so sudden, worse than the last time.' A big rotund man in his late fifties, his florid face laced with broken veins and with the dark brown eyes of a pleading spaniel, nodded in her direction. 'What can we do for her?' Farmer Heron asked.

Isobel watched the doctor examine his patient then stand back and frown. 'Not a lot I'm afraid, apart from make her comfortable. I did warn her the last time.'

'I know,' the wretched farmer cried, 'but you know what she was like she would never slow down, always something else to do.'

The doctor nodded his head. 'We'll just have to wait and see when, she comes around. Nurse here will stay with her. You and I will have a word downstairs.'

Later the doctor returned to Thornbury to attend morning surgery leaving Isobel behind to care for the dying woman. Just before noon Hazel Heron died in her sleep with her husband by her bed.

During his second visit the doctor said, 'She's gone, I'm afraid,' as he draped the sheet carefully over the pale face and sighed.

Isobel knew he hated to lose a patient, even a one so hopelessly lost as this one was before they had arrived.

He laid a hand on the farmer's shoulder then he and Isobel quietly left the room.

Downstairs they checked that neighbours and friends had gathered to help the farmer then took their leave.

It was a watercolour of a day with a weak sun poking from between low clouds. There was a heavy feeling in the car as they drove back to the village. Isobel was dropped off at her door and as she turned to go in a man in uniform walked up the street towards her.

'Alan,' she sighed.

He walked up and placed an arm around her shoulders as they walked down the path to the door together. Over the following hours they talked and ate, and laughed at Churchill's antics. They listened to music and danced around the living room as Alan showed her the latest dance steps. She teased him about girlfriends and he asked her when she was going to find a man and settle down.

'Never,' she laughed. 'We'll grow old together, just you, me and Churchill.'

He grew serious then. 'No,' he said, 'I want you to marry and have children so that I can come over and spoil them.'

'And teach them bad habits and secret ways to annoy me! No thank you.' She reached over to grab the passing Churchill and lift him onto her knee to hide the emotion threatening to overwhelm her.

It was over in a flash, the few hours they'd shared, as she stood on the doorstep and watched him walk away down the street. He turned at the bus stop and waved to her before boarding the bus. She felt a cold shiver run through her as the bus pulled away and trundled off down the road.

*   *   *

Work was never far away to take her mind off personal worries, but for some reason it didn't help over the following few days. Was it a premonition that made her feel so fearful, she wondered, and prayed that she might be wrong. Several times she found her mind drifting and had to snap back to attention when asked for help or a reply when she had not heard the question.

She asked about Duncan Lewis whenever the opportunity arose, but he was still in a coma the doctor informed her. That made her think about Jack and she decided that she would make the effort to visit him on her next day off.

Friday morning arrived and she was covered for the weekend. The weather was sunny but still with a nip in the air as she set out for the early bus into Rennington. From there she would catch another bus to Morpeth. The

45

hospital was a large old house and as Isobel approached the tall iron gates that stood permanently open, an ambulance passed her and turning in through the gates continued on up the drive.

Isobel followed, admiring the open lawns and groups of different varieties of trees. As she got closer the park-like grounds gave way to sculptured gardens. She climbed the four stone steps up to the thick oak doors.

The doors stood open to the spring sunshine and inside the wide hall with its stone floor and wood panelled walls was a monstrous hearth, its grate filled with daffodils and greenery. A middle-aged lady sat at a desk in the corner. She looked up and smiled as Isobel approached.

'Can I help you?'

'I have come to visit Jack Lewis.'

'Is he expecting you?'

'No, should I have rung?'

The woman smiled and shook her head. 'That's not necessary, we simply like to keep a list of patients' visitors. Are you family?'

'No, I'm the district nurse that was treating his father.'

She looked up then. 'Ah yes, how is Mr Lewis? He's in the Royal Hospital, I understand?'

Isobel was surprised that they were aware of Jack's father's condition, but, she admonished herself, of course they would be, seeing as his accident would be playing on Jack's mind and possibly hindering his recovery. 'No better, I'm afraid. He's still in a coma.'

'How sad,' she said nodding her head sympathetically. 'I shall have someone come and show you over to the west wing,' she said, lifting up a telephone. 'They are usually over there this time of the morning.'

A young woman in a white uniform arrived, and after a quick word with the woman at the desk turned and asked Isobel to follow her.

Isobel followed her through a door at the back of the hall and down a long passage. Off this passage were several doors and it was the farthest door that she opened and went through. It led into a long narrow room containing a variety of tables and chairs, bookshelves and a cupboard. The tables were scattered with newspapers and ashtrays, two men sat over an unfinished game of chess, while a third was busy trying to turn the page of a book with his elbow.

Tall windows led out onto a stone veranda whose carved balustrade overlooked a beautiful garden with gentle walkways and arbours. Water features and statuary abounded. Several other men were walking or being pushed in the gardens, some with visitors, some with just a nurse, some sitting alone perhaps waiting for their visitors, Isobel thought.

The nurse was distracted by a group of men

47

sitting just outside the window, as Isobel gazed around looking for Jack. She came back and taking Isobel's arm pointed to a tall hedge beyond the water fountain. 'The boys say he walked over that way. So if you will forgive me I am wanted elsewhere.'

'Of course, thank you.' There was fluttering in her stomach as she set out across the garden. Was she doing the right thing, coming to see him? Perhaps her visit would do more harm than good. Why had she come, she asked herself, it wasn't as if he was her patient. She walked around the pond with the serpent fountain in its centre and crossed to the arbour gateway in the tall hedge.

He was sitting perfectly still, staring ahead at nothing in particular. She hesitated to interrupt. Beyond the walkway was a rose garden but as yet there were no flowers. It was hard to see what attraction the place had to draw anyone up to this part of the garden, but Isobel knew that its very isolation was what would appeal to Jack.

She stepped out from the end of the hedge and went to sit on the first bench. It felt cold through her thin skirt. She remained quiet waiting for him to break the silence. She thought he was going to completely ignore her until he asked, 'What are you doing here?'

'I came to see you.'

'Why?'

'I wanted to know why you decided to

48

return here.'

'That's no business of yours.'

'I know, but I feel responsible.' She fidgeted, trying to ease the discomfort of the seat.

He turned to look at her then. 'Responsible, how?'

'Your mother told me that it was after our last meeting that you decided to return to the hospital and I thought that something I had said had made you think that . . .'

'I can't even remember what you said, but it certainly did not influence my decision.'

'I see, then why did you come back, you were making good progress.'

'You mean until I killed my father!' he snapped.

'That's rubbish.' His guilt and pain were obvious to her and her concern was genuine. 'Something made you freeze, OK, that's medical, not deliberate. Are the doctors here any closer to knowing why you froze?'

He was silent a long time. He made a constant washing motion with his hands between his knees. 'If they had found him sooner, he would have been alive.'

Isobel chewed her lower lip. 'He is alive, Jack, and you don't know how long he lay there. It could have been only a matter of minutes and I doubt it would have made much difference, it was the blow to his head that did the damage.'

'They tell me it was shock that made me freeze and that it shouldn't happen again.'

'Well that's good news, isn't it?'

'It changes nothing,' he said.

Isobel's heart lay heavy in her chest. 'When do you intend going home?'

'I belong here as long as they will have me.'

'But why, you have a perfectly good home whether you help out on the farm or not.'

He turned on her full of anger. 'Because I belong here. Look around you, what do you see. Pieces of men, lots and lots of pieces of men. If you fit them all together like a jigsaw you might get one or two whole ones. Now leave me alone.'

'I pray every night that my brother will return safe and well and if, heaven forbid, he should end up here some day, then I shall pray harder still that he continues to fight, as we all, are fighting this terrible war.' She stood up and made to leave, her heart heavy with his rejection of her.

A SOLUTION TO BOBBY'S PROBLEMS

That evening, unable to settle, Isobel went out to *The Apple*, one of the two public houses in the village. Sylvia Brown, the publican's wife, was a friend of hers and while she couldn't stand Sylvia's husband, the over-jolly, roving-eyed Stan, a quiet drink with Sylvia might help to put her mind back onto an even keel.

The place was busy and Sylvia was serving behind the bar but she managed to indicate to Isobel that she should go through into the lounge. After a while Sylvia came in to join her and sat down placing a sweet sherry in front of Isobel.

'Jeanie's standing in for me,' she explained to Isobel's anxious enquiry. 'Rough day?'

Isobel nodded. 'Rough few days.'

'I heard about Duncan and poor Hazel Heron.'

Isobel sipped at her drink. 'It's Alan I'm worried about, Syl,' she said, replacing her glass on the table and twisting it around by the stem.

'Why Alan, what's happened?'

'Nothing really,' she looked up smiling. 'It's just his usual chat was different this time. More serious, if you know what I mean.'

'Well that's natural isn't it, under the circumstances. He's doing a dangerous job and there is only the two of you. He's bound to be worrying about you should anything happen to him.'

'I know, but today I went to visit another man, a pilot like Alan, but bombers. His injuries are severe but it's the way he has died inside his head that bothers me.'

'A friend?' Sylvia asked.

'No.'

'A patient?'

Isobel shook her head impatiently. 'No, well yes sort of, he's the son of a patient.'

'Why?'

Isobel looked up at her friend, a small frown between her brows. 'Why, what?'

'Why especially this man?'

'I don't understand.'

Her friend leant across the table and placed a hand over Isobel's. 'How often have you told me that you cannot afford to let personal feelings interfere with your work and yet here you are and for some reason you have mixed your concern for Alan and this man together and it is causing you distress. So who is he and what does he mean to you?'

Isobel stared at her friend for several minutes then slowly began to shake her head in denial. 'It's not personal, Syl, it's just such a waste and I know I could never allow that to happen to Alan.'

Sylvia took a drink from her glass and avoided her companion's gaze. They continued to chat about other things until Isobel stood up to go.

Her heart was still heavy as she entered the cottage on her return and she missed Churchill's disapproving gaze as he waited expectantly for his welcome. When it didn't come he stalked past her with his tail in the air and took occupancy of the most comfortable chair by the fire.

It had eased her worries just talking to Sylvia even if her friend's misunderstanding of the situation had rattled her somewhat. But Sylvia had her own worries and Isobel had been reluctant to burden her further. There was a hand written message on the living room table that read: *The Babby's bad. Can you come. Jonny.* With a sigh she reached for her bag.

*   *   *

It was midnight by the time she returned to the cottage once more. Heavy eyed and weary she failed to notice the shadow that passed beyond the kitchen window. Mr Churchill was out doing whatever it was cats did at night.

Dropping her bag on the table she sat down in the nearest chair and eased her hot swollen feet from the restrictions of her shoes, biting her lip as she pressed them to the cold floor.

A shuffling sound had her raise her head. 'Churchill?'

Silence. She toyed with the idea of whether or not to fetch a basin of water to steep her feet in.

A small thud and she cast a concerned glance at the back door. On the point of getting up her breath caught in her throat as she watched the sneck slowly begin to rise.

Seconds later Bobby Dunn fell through the doorway and collapsed on the floor.

The jacket sleeve of his left arm was soaked in blood. Isobel moved swiftly into the living room and taking hold of a large armchair pushed it through into the kitchen where she placed it close to Bobby with its back to the wall. Now she heaved and pulled the half conscious man into the chair.

Taking a pair of scissors from her bag she proceeded to cut away the sleeve of his jacket, not without a little mild protest from her patient.

'What on earth happened to you, Bobby?'

'Cut m' self,' he mumbled.

'I can see that, but what were you doing . . . oh my lord,' she said as she revealed the large gash on his lower arm that had avoided the main blood vessel by a mere hair's breadth.

He started to cry, from weakness and shock, she realised as she got to work. Half-an-hour later, stitched and bandaged, he rested peacefully in the armchair wrapped in a blanket after two mugs of hot sweet tea. She decided he would in all probability sleep until morning so leaving him where he was she climbed wearily up to her own bed.

He was still asleep when she came down the following morning. Moving into the kitchen she put the kettle on to boil and scrambled two eggs in a pan when she heard him moving about in the other room.

'My arm aches,' he complained, coming up behind her.

'You're lucky you have one,' she replied, 'the bathroom's in there,' she said, pointing to the opposite end of the kitchen.

He stumbled off to the bathroom and a few minutes later there was the most horrific crash. Isobel, raising her eyes heavenward, hurried over to the door and knocked. 'Bobby, are you all right in there? What was that noise?'

'Nothing, thing fell off the wall, that's all.'

Isobel groaned. What was she going to do with him, she couldn't let him go back up into the woods on his own or that arm would be septic in no time. Yet she couldn't keep him here, someone was bound to find out, then he would be whisked back off to the workhouse.

She should turn him in for his own good, it was her duty, she told herself over and over, yet somehow she knew there had to be another answer.

She left Bobby back in the armchair with Churchill, who had surprised her by taking to the old man, on his lap and listening to the wireless.

*   *   *

It was when she decided to visit Joyce Lewis that the idea gradually began to take shape.

'I'm sorry there is still no word about Duncan.'

The woman gave her a weak smile and Isobel could have sworn that Joyce Lewis looked thinner than ever.

'How are things working out on the farm? Are your neighbours still helping with the heavy work?'

They were sitting in the kitchen drinking tea. 'Everyone has been very kind, but the lad has gone now and Ned is doing what he can, but I'm thinking of leaving and moving into town to be near Duncan.'

'Has there been no word from Jack?'

'No, nothing, I get lonely in this big house with no-one to look after. It's not the same working all hours and no-one to share it with.'

'I'm surprised the War Office hasn't sent you some help.'

With a shrug of her thin shoulders she pulled open the table drawer. It was stuffed with envelopes and papers. 'I never was one for the bookwork you see. Duncan did all that. I kept thinking he would be home soon and could sort it out then.'

'Look, do you think you could sort this lot if you had more help with the farm work?'

'I suppose I'll have to eventually.'

Isobel laid her hand over the other woman's hand and smiled. 'I have a favour to ask, that might be helpful. I know that help is hard to find at the moment with all the men away fighting. But I have someone in desperate need of being taken care of. He's a big strong fellow and I'm sure he could be a help around the place when he recovers. I understand you wouldn't want him in the house, but I'm sure he would be perfectly comfortable in the barn. If you could feed him and keep an eye on him for me I would be very grateful.'

'Who is it?'

Isobel chewed her lips, then closing her eyes, took the bull by the horns and said, 'It's Bobby Dunn.'

'Where's he from?'

Isobel stared across the table unwilling to believe that Mrs Lewis hadn't heard of Bobby. He's a tramp who's been living rough. He had an accident and is hurt. He's all right now, but I don't want him returning to his old life until his wound is healed properly.'

'Well he'd be welcome if he won't mind giving me a hand now and again when he can.'

'He's a bit slow so you might have to tell him what you want him to do.'

'That's all right, Nurse. There's more than him a bit slow around here.'

Isobel couldn't believe her good fortune as she continued on her rounds. If she could only impress on Bobby that there was to be no drinking and he was to do everything Mrs Lewis told him and in return he would be well looked after.

'Don't want to be looked after, can look after m'self.' Bobby ambled over to the sink, turned on the tap and holding his hand beneath the running water slurped it up into his mouth.

'Mrs Lewis is in real need of help, Bobby. She says you can stay in her nice warm barn and she makes suet puddings and caraway cake. You'll like looking after the animals, won't you?' Isobel was near to tears of frustration. Bobby was being more difficult than she had ever imagined. If he didn't take to this idea then he would just go off back up onto the moors.

'Animals never did me no harm.' Mr Churchill was winding himself around Bobby's legs and purring so loudly he was clearly audible. The cat had attached himself to this new person. 'Have my own place.'

Isobel held her breath expecting his next words to say, 'To be going back to'.

'Don't like killing animals.'

'You won't need to kill these animals just look after them for Mrs Lewis.'

He came back to the armchair, the cat at his heels.

'There won't be any drink,' she said in a firm tone of voice.

'No drink.'

'No.'

'Take the cat,' he said, as Mr Churchill jumped up onto his knee and made himself at home.

'Oh, I'm sure they have lots of cats at the farm.' Startled Isobel had a sudden vision of her darling pet mixing with the feral cats at Pine Tree.

58

'Take the cat,' Bobby repeated, 'he likes me.'

Let him take him, she thought, he'll come back home.

The next afternoon she and Bobby set off for Pine Tree Farm with Churchill sitting happily in the basket on the front of the bicycle. When they arrived Mrs Lewis made them welcome with tea and bran cake. Then she took them over to the barn to show them where Bobby could stay. In a corner piled with hay she had placed a sleeping bag.

'The pump and toilet are in the yard,' she said, 'and you're welcome to eat in the kitchen with me.'

Isobel could see trouble ahead if she tried to alter Bobby's hygiene habits. Churchill had followed them into the barn and at the sound of Mrs Lewis's voice a couple of feral cats appeared from behind some stacked equipment and made to cross the floor towards them. Churchill immediately went into defence mode and growled deep in his throat.

Bobby turned to Isobel and said, 'Need my things.'

Isobel nodded. 'You stay here, I'll get them for you.'

'No, I'll get them, my things.'

'Yes I know, but if you are seen in the village they will send you back to the workhouse.'

'No.' He shouted angrily. 'No workhouse.'

Mrs Lewis was becoming alarmed. 'What's all this about the workhouse? I thought you said he was a tramp.'

Cursing silently Isobel tried to calm the woman. 'He was until some people burnt down his shelter and left him homeless. He was taken to hospital but walked out as he didn't like being in an enclosed place, so they sent him to the workhouse, but again he left preferring to live rough until he came to my house for help with an axe wound. I just want to see him safe until his wound heals.'

Bobby had quietened now and was making shushing noises at the farm cats. Mrs Lewis was watching him.

'All right,' she said quietly, 'I'll ask Tom, my neighbour's boy, to take him and the horse and cart and fetch his things over tomorrow.'

*   *   *

Isobel watched for Mr Churchill's return every day, but as time passed it became obvious that he had changed his alliance. At surgery one evening Doctor Turnbull told her that there had been news of Duncan Lewis.

'He's recovered consciousness and they're hopeful that he will be fine.'

'Has his wife been informed?'

'One would hope so, Nurse. If that fool, Burns, delivered the message this morning.'

Isobel raised her eyebrows. Constable Burns was a very conscientious policeman. Most particular in upholding the law and a good friend to most of the villagers.

'Why wouldn't he, Doctor?'

'Silly fellow got himself blown up yesterday.'

A cry left Isobel's lips.

'Oh, don't make a fuss, girl he's quite all right, unlike the other poor fellow. It's the blast you see, three of them are walking along the street when a bomb goes off higher up the road. Took the prisoner clean out from between them. Left Burns with just the empty handcuffs dangling from his wrist. He was shaken up, told him to take two aspirin and take the day off, but not half-an-hour later he's out on the street again chasing those Cooper boys.'

Isobel decided there and then that she would call in to Pine Tree Farm the following day during her rounds. It was another day of sun, showers and blustery winds when Isobel arrived at the farm gate and called for Joyce Lewis.

The geese were in a bad temper and there was no way she was going through that gate unescorted. But it wasn't Joyce who came to her aid, but Bobby. With surprise she could see he'd had a hair cut and his clothes were clean. He didn't need the broom, simply shooed them away with a wave of his hand.

'You're looking very well, Bobby,' she said,

as she entered the kitchen. Joyce Lewis was lifting a steaming pie from the oven and she turned and placed it carefully on the already laden table.

'My goodness you've had a busy day, Mrs Lewis, by the look of it.'

'I have that, Nurse, but my Duncan is coming home and he will need feeding up and this chap can put some food away as well,' she said, smiling to where Bobby was sifting himself down at the table.

'I heard the good news about Duncan. You will be going in to see him soon I expect, give him my regards won't you.'

'I will that, Nurse, and I'm to get a lift tomorrow with the milk lorry.'

'How's your arm, Bobby?' Isobel asked.

'Better,' he replied, eyeing up the pie.

'Have you been helping Mrs Lewis?'

'Oh aye, Nurse, he's a grand help. I don't know how I managed without him. Will you have a seat and take a cup of tea.'

As Isobel pulled out a chair she surprised a bad tempered scowl from Churchill who was curled up and had obviously been sleeping until his rude awakening. Out of force of habit she refrained from disturbing him, but simply pulled out another chair. He had made no effort to welcome her or show any affection toward her at all and she was rather hurt by his disdain.

'He likes it here,' Bobby mumbled, watching

Mrs Lewis pour out the tea and cut into a large caraway cake. 'Cats don't like village people, like I don't.'

'Well you won't be able to stay here when Mr Lewis comes home so we will have to find somewhere else for you, Bobby.'

'Want to stay here,' he said, spraying crumbs.

Isobel shook her head as she accepted the cup of tea but refused the cake.

'Oh he's no bother, Nurse. I'm sure Duncan won't mind him staying.'

'Told you,' he said, before gulping down tea from the largest blue and white striped pot Isobel had ever seen.

'Well let me know how your visit goes, won't you, Mrs Lewis. I don't suppose you have heard anything of Jack lately.'

'Not since he went down south, no.'

Isobel's attention was pricked and she stared at the woman across the table. 'Down south? He's left the hospital?'

'Oh yes, they sent for him, you see.'

'Who sent for him?'

The woman frowned with concentration. 'Some important person in London said they had a job for him. The doctor at the hospital is a friend of his and he recommended him.'

Isobel could hardly believe her own ears.

'He said not to worry, he was feeling much better and he would be home soon.'

'Well I'm very pleased for you, Mrs Lewis.

So much good news at once. Now I must be on my way.' She waved to Bobby as she cycled back down the track.

With the wind at her back she fair flew the distance to the main road and it took all her time to keep the bike steady. Once pedalling back to the village, however, her mind began to sift through what the farmer's wife had told her.

Was it really possible that Jack Lewis had made a seemingly remarkable turnabout, or was there more to it than he was telling, she wondered. What was this so-called job he'd been offered? By the time she reached the cottage she had convinced herself once more that it was none of her business.

* * *

Macky and some of his friends were standing outside *The Cat and Dog*, when Isobel passed them on the edge of the village. Macky stepped out in front of the bike and grabbed the handlebars. 'A word, Nurse,' he said.

'Let go of my bike this minute, Joseph Mackenzie.'

'Just asking about Bobby Dunn, Nurse,' he said, dropping his hand from the bike.

'What about him?' She was tired and in no mood for Macky and pals.

'We hear you have him tucked in up at Pine Tree. Mrs Lewis is all on her own up there,

Nurse. Anything could happen to her.'

'It had better not, Macky. Bobby has been a great help to Mrs Lewis, cleaned himself up and doesn't drink any more, so you leave well alone. Anyway, Duncan is on the road to recovery and it won't be long until he is home.'

'Glad to hear that, Nurse.' A chorus of *ayes* came from his group of friends. 'Good sort is Duncan Lewis, shame about that lad of his though.' The men's talk followed her down the main street.

It always riled her to hear them picking away at people, some of whom had never done or said a word against anyone in their lives. They were just like a group of schoolyard bullies.

She felt like banging their heads together. She was still in a mood when she tripped over something on the doorstep of the cottage. Banging her bag down on the bench top she went to retrieve the shovel to sweep up whatever had been deposited on the step. Swinging the shovel downward it stopped mere inches from the bedraggled cat.

'What on . . .' flinging the shovel to one side she dropped to her knees beside Churchill. That she even recognised him was a miracle, for he was a tatty mess of blood so crumpled she was afraid to lift him.

Swiftly she stepped back into the kitchen and prepared a temporary bed of an old box she kept kindling in, stuffed with newspaper and covered with a tea towel.

With afternoon calls to make she was torn between the cat and her patients. Work won and placing the box in a cosy corner by the fire she left on her rounds. All afternoon she worried about him and when at last she returned to the cottage expecting to find he had died, she was greeted by an empty box.

Calling softly to him she searched in the kitchen, around cupboards, under table and sink, but there was no response so she moved on into the living room. With her eyes at floor level she nearly missed him, sitting curled up in his favourite chair. He had made a fantastic recovery and looked none the worse for his adventure until he stood up to stretch when Isobel quickly reached into her bag for her scissors and with a snip cut the last thread holding his tail to his body.

He stayed until evening, ate a large supper then disappeared into the night.

*   *   *

Isobel attended morning surgery before her rounds and shared evening surgery with the nurse from the next village. This morning when she arrived at the surgery she found the door locked and a queue of people waiting patiently outside. Thinking the doctor had slept in or had a sudden call-out and gone without her, she banged on the door.

Normally if he had been called away there would be a message on the door, but this morning there was nothing. She looked in the window and rattled on the glass.

The queue was getting restless. 'We've tried that, Nurse,' a woman standing with a little boy beside her said.

'Can't raise the housekeeper either,' said a tall, thin man with a hacking cough.

'Timmy,' she said, pulling a schoolboy, always looking for a reason not to attend school, away from his nervous mother. 'Run round to Constable Burns and ask him to come to the doctor's house, be quick,' she said, giving him a gentle push in the right direction. The boy ran off.

A few minutes later the boy arrived back with the policeman in tow. He stopped in front of Isobel and glanced along the queue of waiting people. 'What can I do for you, Nurse?'

'We can't get in, Constable. Neither the doctor nor Mrs Holland are answering the door.'

'Well obviously they are both out,' he said, stepping forward to bang on the door.

'I don't think so, not during surgery hours.'

'Hmm,' he said, rubbing a hand across his chin. He stepped back and looked up at the windows. 'Hmm,' he said again. 'I think we had better get Mackenzie up here with his ladder. Off you go, lad,' he said turning to Timmy.

The boy ran off once more and one or two of the people waiting decided to come back later and wandered away.

'Rum business,' the constable said to Isobel. 'What do you think has happened, Nurse?'

Isobel shook her head. She had no idea, but she was afraid that something awful must have happened to keep the doctor away from his patients. Then there was the missing housekeeper. A middle-aged woman with no family, who had been taking care of the doctor since before Isobel had come to the village. Where would she have gone? No, Isobel was convinced they were both still in the house.

Macky arrived, sauntering up the hill with his ladder on his shoulder. Timmy was walking along side him chattering nineteen to the dozen.

'Get a move on, man,' Constable Burns shouted. 'We have an emergency here.'

'All right, all right.' Macky came forward and propped his ladder against the wall. 'Where's the fire?'

'No fire, but the doctor and Mrs Holland aren't answering the door and may be in trouble.'

'Why didn't you break a window? I was in the middle of my breakfast.'

'Never mind that now, get up that ladder and tell us what you can see.'

Grumbling Macky ascended the ladder and a second later shouted that he could see

68

nothing. 'There's no-one there.'

'Right then, come back and go to the next one.'

There was a lot of shuffling around as the queue dispersed and some of the men helped Macky while others rested against the garden wall.

'The doc's still asleep,' yelled Macky from the top of the ladder at the second window. He rattled on the glass. Then in a worried voice, 'He's not moving, Burns.'

'Can you get the window open?' The constable shouted, but he was too late as a crash and a shower of glass had him duck out of the way.

Macky was through the window and coughing and spluttering when he poked his head out of the now opened window and shouted. 'It's a gas leak.'

'Get the door,' the constable shouted back.

Macky's head nodded and withdrew.

'Nurse, with me,' the constable called as Macky could be heard unlocking the front door. With handkerchiefs over their noses they dashed into the hall and up the stairs where they ran from room to room opening windows. Others had followed them up the stairs and were together carrying the doctor and Mrs Holland outside.

Isobel was doing the best she could for them while someone else had run to ring for the ambulance. Doctor Turnbull was the first to show signs of recovery and soon Isobel had to fight to get him to lie still. He coughed and choked his way back to consciousness, his voice faint and raspy, yet the words were as strong as ever.

'Where the devil am I? Get me up you stupid woman.'

Leaving him to the constable, Isobel returned her attention to the housekeeper. The woman was still unconscious and Isobel worked furiously to breathe some life into her. She was gratefully relieved when the ambulance turned up and Mrs Holland was lifted inside. Doctor Turnbull flatly refused to go and said he would take morning surgery in the Nurse's House. So Isobel took him home and persuaded him to sit in the armchair while she made him a cup of tea. Five minutes later he was fast asleep.

JACK RETURNS TO THE VILLAGE

On a warm June afternoon Isobel was cycling up the valley when a black Austin car passed her and came to a halt at the bottom of the track leading up to Pine Tree Farm.

Curious she slowed down and dropped her foot to the road to steady the bike. She was on her way to the farm to check up on Duncan, who had been home for a fortnight. So who is this, she wondered, screwing up her eyes against the sun. One man had got out and the car pulled away and continued on up the road. The man in a dark suit and trilby hat pulled low down on his forehead walked off up the track. He held a stick in his hand and walked with a limp.

'Jack,' she said to herself. Kicking the pedal round she took off at a rare rate and wasn't far behind him as she approached the farm gate. Jack was on the point of entering the kitchen when she called out to him.

Dropping the bike against the wall she went to open the gate as the geese came, running back from hissing at Jack ready to attack their next victim. Two visitors at one time seemed to have worked them into a frenzy and Isobel froze as they rushed towards her with their necks stretched and their beaks open.

Jack had turned back with his hand still on the door sneck. When he saw her predicament his mouth tweaked in a lopsided smile. He walked back across the yard scattering the geese as he went.

Gratefully, Isobel squeezed through the gate and walked back with him. 'Thank you. Are they expecting you?'

'No, I had the offer of a lift and took it.' His flat frame had filled out more and the dark blue eyes flickered with life. Gone was the death mask. Someone or something had healed him. He would in all probability never

71

lose his ghosts, but at least he was alive now and anything was possible. Isobel felt a warm glow inside her for whatever or whoever had brought about the change.

When they walked into the kitchen it was empty and Isobel could have laughed at the anti-climax to their arrival.

'Duncan knows I'm coming so he can't be far away.' There was a lovely smell of food and a plate of scones and a bran cake stood on the table set for three.

Jack raised his eyebrows questioningly. 'Are you staying for tea?'

Isobel felt the blood rush to her face. 'No. They have a helper on the farm. He came when your mother was on her own and your father kept him on. Are you home to stay?'

'Yes, but who . . .'

Isobel opened her mouth to tell him about Bobby, then, changed her mind. His gaze wandered around the room then came back to her face and his dark eyes studied her grey ones as the door opened and Joyce Lewis came in.

'Jack,' she stood open mouthed in the doorway. Then she remembered herself and addressed the nurse. 'Sorry, Nurse, but it's such a surprise, Duncan will be back in a minute, he's taken to walking around the farm each day. I don't think he trusts old Ned, to take care of it. Bobby's with him. Eh Jack, he'll be so glad you're back. Why didn't you let us know you were coming?'

There was a lot of shuffling beyond the door and Duncan and Bobby arrived. Bobby took one look at Isobel and left. About to go after him Joyce stopped her. 'He's feeling guilty,' she said with a smile.

'Why, what about?'

'The cat,' she said, 'followed him to the next farm when I sent him with a message. They have terriers, I forgot to warn him and they killed the cat.'

Isobel understood now and smiled back. 'Oh no they didn't, he came home and he's fine now.'

'Really? Oh he will be pleased.'

Meanwhile a slower Duncan was greeting his son. 'Where have you been, lad? What have you been up to, eh?'

Jack helped his father into a chair then sat down next to him. 'I've been given some administrative work at the Hall. I'll be living in, but it's local so I'll be up to see you from time to time.'

'At the Hall?'

'Yes, they have turned it into a POW camp.'

Duncan was rubbing his chin. He seemed to be having trouble taking in this news.

Isobel was watching them as they talked, concerned that Jack didn't as yet understand that his father needed time to assimilate changes.

'You're not at the hospital any more, that's

73

good. You're home now right?'

Jack sat back in his seat and threw a searching glance at Isobel.

Joyce bustled forward. 'Off you go with Nurse, Dad. Jack will still be here when you come back.' She looked towards her son for confirmation. Jack nodded.

Isobel moved towards the passage door and Duncan followed her.

When she had renewed the dressing on his ulcer and checked him through his daily exercises, she and Duncan returned to the kitchen where she washed her hands and got ready to leave. Bobby hadn't returned, but Joyce promised to tell him that Churchill was alive and well but minus a tail. As Joyce made to escort her over the yard, Jack stood up and said he wanted a word, so they left the kitchen together.

The geese were at the far end of the yard and didn't bother them. They walked in silence until they reached the gate.

'Is he going to recover?'

'He has recovered, the rest will just take time.'

His mouth twisted into an ugly line. 'What a pat answer, are you all trained to repeat the same phrases?' he asked scornfully.

'What do you want me to say, Jack? That I don't know. He has medication and exercises and with luck and hard work they should help him make a full recovery. That he is ever going

74

to be the same man he was before the accident, then, no I don't believe he is.'

The look on his face frightened her, as the grip on her arm tightened. Then just as suddenly his hand fell away and she was free, but she didn't walk away. 'It was never your fault, Jack. He doesn't blame you and neither should you blame yourself.'

He gave a heavy sigh and relaxed. 'It was hard seeing him like that.'

'No harder than it was for him when he first saw you,' she said softly.

Nodding his head he said, 'You're right of course, the table turns yet again.'

'For all of us, Jack,' she said, thinking of Alan flying one mission after another.

*   *   *

She was visiting Sylvia in *The Apple* the next time she saw Jack. 'I didn't know they had changed the use of the old hall. What happened to the Crombies? I had quite a shock when the Lewises told me.'

'Oh yes, they've turned it into a POW camp. The Crombies have moved into the lodge.'

'Well prisoners or not, they should be comfortable enough in there.'

'They're not in the Hall itself, they're being billeted in the grounds.'

'Well if they are sending any of them out to work they might do worse than send someone up to Pine Tree, they could do with some extra help up there. Jack Lewis has been given a job at the Hall.'

'No!' Sylvia looked shocked. 'I thought something was up when he was in here the other night. We never saw hide nor hair of him before. So he's not back living at home then.'

Isobel wasn't one to gossip but she couldn't resist putting Sylvia in the picture. 'No, he's living in at the job, so I suppose that means the Hall.'

Sylvia said, 'There're several staff up there and always one or two of them in here of a night.'

Over the top of the snug bar Isobel could just see Jack and an older man sitting in deep conversation in the far corner of the men's bar. 'I wonder what this job of his entails?'

Sylvia took a sip of her drink before saying, 'Whatever it is, it's pretty important because the others heed him when he gives orders.'

'Do they now.' Isobel couldn't deny that she was curious to know what or who had caused this transformation from the bitter sick man of earlier. She looked up and caught Sylvia watching her, and laughing shook her head.

The door opened and more soldiers piled into the bar. There was a lot of laughing and joking and Sylvia stood up. 'I'd better help out,' she said, and turned back to the bar. Before Isobel could finish her drink some of the soldiers wandered into the snug looking for a seat.

'Mind if we sit down?' a deep voice enquired.

Isobel looked all the way up over brass buttons to a round baby face too young for the voice. She smiled and nodded. 'I was on the point of leaving anyway.'

Heavy boots clunked under the table as two of them took a seat. 'Oh please don't go, have a drink, what can I get you?'

Babyface's friend was on his feet, deep brown eyes staring into her face, challenging her to stay.

'No really, I must be on my way.'

'Hubby waiting for you, is he? An extra ten minutes isn't going to hurt, now, is it. Come on, what's it to be. Shandy, gin? No, let me guess, I bet you're a sweet sherry girl, am I right? One sweet sherry, please,' he shouted across to Sylvia.

Sylvia glanced over and Isobel shook her head.

He had turned the chair and was sitting astride it with his arms across the back leaning into her face. Babyface had become distracted by a girl at the next table. Isobel finished her drink and rose to her feet.

'We're spilling blood and guts for you, doll. The least you could do was give a chap some attention.'

'Goodnight,' she said, leaving the table. She gave Sylvia a little wave and made her way to the door.

*   *   *

A chill wind was blowing down the valley, and here and there an odd slap and bang from a loose garden gate or somebody's bin lid echoed in the dying evening.

Hurrying up the main street with her coat wrapped tightly around her and her mind dwelling on the apparent new Jack Lewis, she exchanged greetings with the shadowy figures that came and went along the road. Some of them called out when they recognised her, others passing silently onward.

Coming to her gate she let herself through and started up the path before she realised there was someone behind her. At first mistaking him for Alan she turned back to him 'Alan?' When he didn't reply she hesitated.

'Can I help you?'

'You can ask me in for a drink.'

As soon as he spoke she recognised the soldier from the pub. 'I don't think so, on your way before . . .' she got no further before she was grabbed by the arm and dragged into the deeper shadows of the house. 'If you don't want me to scream my head off you better let go.'

She felt the weight of his body pushing her against the wall as the sour smell of his breath invaded her face. On the point of fighting back

78

he was suddenly wrenched from her and hurled to one side. Words snapped and crackled in the air then he was gone and she was left facing Jack Lewis.

'He won't be bothering you again, you have my word.'

'How did you know?'

'Sylvia.'

'Well thank you for coming to the rescue, if I'd had my uniform on I doubt if he would have bothered me, he'd just had too much to drink.'

'You're shaking,' he said with concern.

'Fright, that's all.' She peeled herself away from the wall and turned to open the door. 'Please, would you mind taking a look,' she stepped back from the door and turned expectantly towards him. She didn't see his expression but sensed his reluctance. Then he moved past her and entered the house.

She heard him check the blackout blinds then the lights went on. A few moments followed then he was back on the doorstep again.

'It's clear.'

'Thank you.' He was about to turn away and walk down the path when she hesitated on the threshold and asked, 'Would you like a coffee?'

'Won't that keep you awake?'

'No more than a call out. I only have Camp, I'm afraid,' she said, as he followed her into the cottage.

'I couldn't help noticing how much improved your walking was,' she said as they sat one on either side of the hearth.

'Always the nurse,' he said, with a lift of his lips. 'The face isn't so red either, though the leg is still tin,' he said, rapping it with the stick he still carried.

Come on Isobel she thought, keep off the personal. 'How's the job?'

His long legs were stretched out in front of him as he gazed into the fire and made no reply. She began to think he had fallen asleep. But then he moved restlessly in the chair. 'It's not what I would have wished to be doing, but it's something I suppose. Typical desk work, seeing that everything runs smoothly, that sort of thing.'

'Will the prisoners be allowed out of the camp?'

'Some of them will work on local farms, in the forestry, and on the roads, others will work here in the camps doing whatever it takes to make themselves self sufficient.'

'So what are the chances of your parents getting some help up at Pine Tree?'

He cocked an eyebrow at her. 'Are you always so interested in your patients' welfare?'

'Always.'

'Then I suppose I should be grateful you were never my nurse.' Isobel winced inside and fell silent.

Eventually he put down his cup and stood up. 'Thank you for the coffee,' he said.

Isobel followed him to the door. With his hand on the latch he swung back to face her. 'I'm sorry,' he said, 'you didn't deserve that, you tried to help.' Then he was gone.

The shakes were back as, ignoring the dirty coffee cups, she pulled her chair closer to the fire and wrapped her arms around herself What was it about the man, why did she care what happened to him? What was it to her whether he thought well of her or not?

*　　　*　　　*

Mrs Crombie, a local magistrate, had been put in charge of the Land Army girls and arrived at *The Apple* the following day with two of her girls. They were to help out at Pine Tree Farm at long last.

One of the girls turned out to be Brenda Douglas, a young relative of Sylvia's. The girls were to be housed at the pub as there was no room for them at the farm. Bicycles had been found for them and these were taken down from the boot of the Crombie family's Bentley and stored amid the beer barrels.

Sylvia hadn't seen her young cousin for some time, she admitted to Isobel. 'She's from Newcastle. She was a sickly baby and my aunt always spoilt her disgracefully, so heaven alone knows how she is going to manage to work on a farm where the work is so heavy and tiring.'

'I'll tell Mrs Lewis to keep an eye on her. Though,' she said, turning to where Brenda and her friend were laughing and giggling at something Norman had said, 'Perhaps it will take more eyes than Mrs Lewis has to watch out for Brenda.'

Norman had taken the girls' cases from them and was leading them away into the pub.

Sylvia looking harassed made her excuses. 'I better go and see them settled,' she said, before hurrying off.

Isobel smiled to herself as she cycled away. She thought perhaps her friend was in for a busy time. The girls' arrival would be welcome news at Pine Tree Farm, she thought as she made her way to morning surgery and propped her bicycle against the wall of the doctor's house. Mrs Holland had recovered from the gas leak and been shocked when she returned from the hospital to discover that the doctor had replaced the old gas oven with a brand new electric one.

'But how am I supposed to know how to use it?' she had complained to Isobel on an earlier visit.

'You'll get used to it, you just have to remember not to try and light it, you just twist the knobs instead.'

'Well I know that,' the good woman huffed. 'What I don't understand is all the figures and how they compare to the gas ones.' So Isobel

82

had set about explaining as best she could.

This morning when she entered the surgery the housekeeper was standing by the doctor's desk with a tray in her hands.

'Join us, Nurse,' the doctor said. 'Mrs Holland's cake is too good to pass up. We'll have tea and cake each morning before surgery from now on.'

Isobel's eyebrows shot up, it wasn't like the doctor to be so generous with his time.

'It's all on account of that new cooker. I should have bought it years ago,' he cried. Mrs Holland's mastery of the new oven or her light-handedness at the baking was never mentioned of course, Isobel noticed, as she gave the housekeeper a sly wink. The cake, without the benefit of sugar, was delicious and set her up fine for the crowded surgery.

When Bobby came through the door the doctor's glasses slipped off his nose and he had to make a sudden snatch to catch them before they fell on the floor. 'What do you want,' he asked.

'Nothing, it's Nurse I've come for.'

Isobel tried to keep a straight face as she glanced across at the doctor who was rubbing furiously at his glasses. 'What is it,' she asked a clean and tidy Bobby, who ignored the doctor and faced Isobel with a worried expression.

'Duncan's bad and Mrs can't help. You have to get Jack.'

'What's the matter with Lewis, man?' the

doctor snapped.

But Bobby was only interested in getting Isobel to fetch Jack.

'I'll go with him and let you know what's happened when I get back,' she said.

The doctor swivelled around in his chair. 'You'd better phone the camp from here seeing as it's an emergency and get young Lewis to come down.'

She crossed to his desk with Bobby dogging her footsteps and picked up the phone. The person who answered told her that Mr Lewis wasn't in, could he phone her back? But Isobel said it wasn't convenient and left a message.

'All right, go go go,' the doctor said flapping his hand at her as she hesitated.

She took Bobby by the arm and left the surgery. 'How did you get here?' she asked, as she turned her bike along the road.

'Walked.'

'Well I'm going to ride up to the farm now, and Jack will come up when he gets my message. So I will see you back at the farm, right?'

'Back at the farm,' he said and nodded his head.

She was in the farmyard when Jack arrived in a long black car and scattered the geese far and wide. Bobby was sitting up beside the driver and by the look on his face thoroughly enjoying the ride. The minute the engine stopped the door shot open and Jack climbed

84

out.

'What's all this about Dad?' he asked Isobel as together they hurried towards the house, but before they entered there was a cry and Joyce Lewis was waving to them from the doorway of the byre.

'Here! Over here, Nurse,' Joyce shouted from the far end of the byre.

By now Jack had arrived and they both made their way along the walkway behind the stalls. At the last stall a strange sight met their eyes. Duncan was lying in the feeding rack with one leg stuck at an angle behind him.

'Lord, help me!' he was shouting at the top of his voice.

'That's all I can get out of him!' cried his harassed-looking wife. 'But when we tried to get him out he screamed something awful. I think his leg must be broken.'

'What were you trying to do in there, Dad? Come on now, stop that shouting this minute or we'll leave you there. Isobel take a look at his leg and see what you think.'

Duncan had quietened at the sound of Jack's voice and Isobel moved forward to take a look at his leg. After a brief inspection she said, 'I don't think it's broken but it is stuck at a difficult angle.'

Jack looked back up the walkway. 'Where's that chap that's supposed to be looking after him?'

'Oh Bobby tried to get him out,' Joyce said,

85

'but when Duncan screamed like that he frightened poor Bobby and he wouldn't try again.'

'Well get him back here, this might take all of us.'

Duncan sounded more like his normal self as he grinned down at Jack and said, 'Eh lad, it's good to see you.'

Isobel had run off to fetch Bobby, who was reluctant to leave the car until she reminded him that they must help Duncan. Once they returned the two men got to work lifting and turning Duncan so that Isobel could manoeuvre the leg into a position to release it from the rails. Once that was done it was just a matter of lifting him free. He was crying like a baby as Bobby carried him out of the byre and across the yard to the house. Joyce held his hand the whole way while Jack and Isobel followed behind.

'Is he going to need further attention?' Jack wanted to know.

'No I shouldn't think so.'

'What the devil was he doing there in the first place?'

'Your mother said he had wanted to help her feed the cows. He had been forking hay into the racks when he accidentally threw his pitchfork through the rails. Apparently he couldn't reach it so instead of coming around to the other side he climbed into the rack to get it, when he turned to climb out he got stuck.'

'Of all the stupid . . .'

Mrs Lewis looked up as they entered the kitchen. 'Bobby is putting him to bed. He'll sleep for a while,' she smiled, 'and then he'll be fine again.'

'Mam he's never going to be fine, we should get you some more help.'

On the point of taking her leave Isobel said, 'There's two Land Army girls just arrived at *The Apple*. I rather think they have been sent here.'

'Oh good,' Joyce sat down and began to rummage in the table drawer, then pulled out a letter. 'Yes, it came a few days ago to tell us we had been allocated help. I told them we couldn't put them up here with only two bedrooms. So will they be staying at *The Apple*, do you know?'

'I should think so, one of them is Sylvia Brown's cousin.'

'That's a great relief. The neighbours are ever so good, but I have felt guilty depending upon them so heavily. Oh Duncan will be pleased. Thank you for coming so swiftly, Nurse,' Joyce said, as Isobel turned once more to the door.

'I'll give you a lift,' Jack said.

Joyce reached up on her toes and kissed his cheek. 'Thanks for coming, love,' she said.

The driver climbed out of the car and stored Isobel's bicycle in the boot, while Jack held the rear door open for her before following her inside. In his seat once more the driver switched on the engine and drove out of the farmyard through the gate Joyce held open for them and down the lane.

'Village High Street,' Jack told the driver and they sat in silence as the car bumped its way down the hill. On the short drive into the village Isobel mulled over what she might say to start a conversation. They had stopped in front of the cottage before, in a desperate rush, she asked, 'Would you like to come in for a coffee?'

With a slow smile he nodded towards the driver and said, 'I think we had both better resume what we were doing when we were called away.'

'Yes, of course how stupid of me.' Embarrassed she lowered her head and turned toward the gate.

'If you are free tomorrow evening perhaps I could buy you a drink.'

She stared back over her shoulder as without waiting for a reply he tapped the driver with his stick and the car moved off along the road back to the camp.

MYSTERY SURROUNDS BOBBY DUNN'S WHEREABOUTS

The following evening Isobel was sorting through her wardrobe trying to decide what she should wear for her date with Jack. It was cold in the bedroom, the little fire rarely lit, and she had changed clothes so often she was covered in goose bumps. At last she conceded that the tartan skirt and green jumper would have to do, after all it would probably be *The Apple*.

He hadn't said when he would pick her up, or where, and she worried about this as she brushed her hair and applied a little more make up than normal.

Downstairs she fussed about checking that there was a handkerchief in her pocket; that her shoes were clean, though she had given them a good polishing earlier. That the best tea cups were ready in case he should come back for coffee later, that there was water in the kettle, and so it went on until there was absolutely nothing else to do and she sat down in front of the fire to wait. Eight o'clock, nine o'clock, ten o'clock, then she turned out the lights and went to bed.

*   *   *

On Saturday evening Sylvia had the night off and she persuaded Isobel to go with her to the village dance. 'You've been looking down all week. What happened, one of your patients died?'

Smiling, Isobel shook her head.

'Well something's up, you're not usually down for long. Come and help me keep an eye on these two young things,' she said, pointing across the room to where Brenda and her friend were entertaining a group of young soldiers. The band was playing a military two step and both girls were whisked onto the floor. Sylvia said something in her ear and disappeared off towards a long trestle table covered in someone's bed sheet and liberally spread with a variety of soft drinks, beer and a large bowl of what was generously called punch, leaving Isobel in direct line of Jack's unflinching gaze.

As he stepped forward clearly indicating his intention of speaking to her Isobel ducked behind a chattering group of villagers, right into the path of Mrs Crombie who promptly whisked her off to help with the organising of the spot prize.

It wasn't until much later that she discovered that Jack had disappeared and so, to Sylvia's consternation, had Brenda.

'Margery, the other girl said she had gone outside for a smoke. Well I've been out there and I can't see her.'

'Don't worry, she'll not be far.'

'It's not how far away she is, it's what she's up to that bothers me,' an anxious Sylvia replied. 'You know what some of these lads are like. Did you see her go off with anyone?'

Isobel looked around the Presbyterian Church Hall. Two thirds of the company were soldiers, the rest mostly local women and girls apart from a group of village lads keeping very much to themselves to one side of the band. 'I'm afraid not.'

'Well keep an eye out for her will you and tell her I'm looking for her if you see her.'

'I'll come and help you find her.' But just at that moment an ex-patient came up and asked her to dance, and Sylvia hurried off. Isobel danced constantly during the second half of the dance, handed from one partner to the next in a whirl of fun and laughter.

Sylvia chased Brenda off and on all night, and as she and Isobel walked home together she complained bitterly that if the girl didn't calm down she, Sylvia, was going to be run off her feet.

Isobel laughed. 'After a hard day's work and cycling back and forth to Pine Tree Farm every day she isn't going to have much energy left for gallivanting, you wait and see.'

Sylvia cut off to *The Apple* and Isobel continued along the street to the cottage. As she drew near to the gate she could see someone standing there waiting for her.

Drawing in a sharp breath she at first thought it to be the soldier who had attacked her once before. But as she neared she recognised Jack.

She came to a halt in front of him.

'I wanted a word with you, but you seemed to be having a good time in there so I decided to wait.'

Her body stiffened and her voice died in her throat as she waited for him to say more.

'May I come in?'

She hesitated, before shrugging her shoulders and pushing open the gate.

He followed her into the cottage kitchen and stood by as she automatically filled the kettle and switched it on. 'I'm sorry about last week, I was due to be off-duty but an emergency came up and I couldn't get away.'

Isobel set out two mugs on the bench. 'No problem. It happens to me all the time.'

Frowning he said, 'Yes, it must be the same for you also, though in your shoes I doubt I would be so gracious.'

She made the cocoa and handed him the other mug. 'Gracious wasn't how I would have described my feelings last Thursday evening.' She moved on into the living room and sat down by the dying fire.

He took the chair opposite without waiting to be invited. 'Then will you let me make amends with an invitation to dinner in Rennington next Saturday.'

She looked at him over the brim of her mug

and with her heart doing a slow drum roll, said, 'Thank you, yes, I'd like that.'

He stayed for half-an-hour and they talked about small inconsequential things. After he left, Isobel sat on in the chair by the fire and dreamt impossible dreams.

*   *   *

It was the following Thursday when Bobby disappeared. 'We dressed the loft in the barn as a bedroom for him because he wouldn't come into the house to sleep. I offered him Jack's old room, but he preferred to be in the barn. I thought he was happy there. He seemed really fond of Duncan, did all sorts of things for him. I don't understand why he would just up and go like that,' Joyce told Isobel when she arrived at the farm on Friday morning to attend to Duncan.

'Did he take anything with him?' Isobel asked the worried woman.

'No, that's what I don't understand. The cat's still here too.'

'Well that's not right, Bobby would never leave Churchill or his belongings. Do you remember the fuss he made when he first came here until he was allowed to go and collect his "things"?'

'So what do you think has happened to him, Nurse?'

'I don't know, Mrs Lewis, but I intend to

find out.'

'Duncan is missing him,' she said, as she led the way into the kitchen. Duncan was waiting for her in his usual chair, looking worried.

'Have the Land Army girls arrived, Duncan?' she asked, watching his expression brighten.

'Aye, with orders to turn the bottom meadow for . . . what was it again?' he asked his wife.

'Potatoes.'

'Oh aye, potatoes.'

'They'll be a grand help, Nurse,' Mrs Lewis said.

'Good. It's about time you had some help.'

'An' that's not all either. We've got a man coming to dig ditches and mend fences. Jack's sending him from the camp. A Pole by the name of Paul. They'll bring him up each morning and collect him at tea-time.'

'Splendid.' Isobel re-dressed Duncan's ulcer and went through his exercises with him before reassuring his wife that she would definitely be making enquires about Bobby.

In the village she headed straight for the Mackenzies' shop. If there was anything suspicious about Bobby's disappearance then it would somehow or other have something to do with Macky Mackenzie. When she asked for him in the shop his wife just shrugged her shoulders. One of her customers piped up as she peered through the tins of broken biscuits spread out along the front of the counter, 'I passed him when I came in, heading for *The Apple,* he was with that Billy Patterson.'

Isobel thanked the woman and headed out the door and up towards the public house.

Sylvia was behind the bar when Isobel entered. The few men already in the bar raised frowning faces at the intrusion of a woman into their domain but when they saw it was the nurse, they retreated back to their own business. Isobel's quick glance told her that Macky wasn't present.

'Have you seen Macky this morning?' she asked Sylvia on her approach to the bar.

'Macky? No why?'

'Bobby Dunn's gone missing from Pine Tree Farm and I'll bet my next salary on it being something to do with Macky. When I get my hands on him . . .'

At that moment the door of the bar opened and in walked Macky and two of his pals. Isobel was at him in a flash, her grandmother's Irish temper flaring.

'What have you done with Bobby Dunn, Macky Mackenzie? And don't give me that surprised innocent look. I warned you what would happen if anything went wrong up at the farm. I know you are behind it and if you don't come along to the Police House right now and tell Constable Burns what you've been up to, I'll get these men to help me drag you there,' she cried pushing him backward with jabs of her fist.

'Hold on,' cried Sylvia, rushing from behind the bar to place herself between her friend and Macky Mackenzie. 'What's he done, what's happened to Bobby Dunn?'

'He's gone, that's what,' a furious Isobel snapped. 'When he was really settled and useful to people who appreciated him. This, this . . . busybody has to go poking his nose into other people's lives because he's such a no gooder,' and here her words failed her.

'Here! You can't talk about me like that!' Macky complained. 'It was none of my doing if that tramp has taken his self off.'

'Of course it was you, why else would he have gone?'

By now the other men in the bar were taking an interest in the proceedings. 'Why don't you tell the nurse what she wants to know,' someone called from the other end of the bar. While Macky's two friends backed up to the door blocking the way of someone else wanting in.

'Aye, you tell the nurse what she wants to know,' a shouted voice backed up the first one.

'I'm telling you, I don't know where he is,' Macky snarled.

When Jack and a group of soldiers pushed their way into the bar the gang of grumbling locals dispersed back to their seats. Jack looked across at the still seething Isobel and raised his eyebrows. A smiling Sylvia draped an arm around the shoulders of her friend and led her away behind the bar and into the back living area.

Norman was there leaning over his books and he looked up clicking his tongue when he saw who it was disturbing him. 'Can't you use the snug for your women's chat? I want to get this down before Brenda gets back tonight,' he looked up grinning. 'Clever little thing, that cousin of yours.'

His grin always made Isobel feel dirty and she turned away with, 'I must be getting back to work. Keep an eye and ear open for me;' she asked her friend, 'anything at all you hear about Bobby, let me know, OK?'

'OK.' Sylvia replied while scowling at her husband.

*　　　*　　　*

'I hear Bobby Dunn has gone missing. Tramps never stay long in the same place.'

Isobel looked up from setting out an ear-syringing tray. I ought to know better, she thought. News in this place needs no voice, it echoes up and down the streets. 'He didn't move on, Doctor, something has happened to him.'

The doctor made a gruff noise and prepared for his next patient who had been hit on the side of his head during a football game and was now complaining of deafness. Young

Timmy kicked up a tremendous fuss so Isobel had to call in his mother to quieten him. When it was over and the doctor was writing out a note for drops, Isobel asked the waiting pair if they had seen anything of Bobby Dunn recently.

The doctor gave Isobel a calculating glance as he handed over the prescription, but she ignored him and listened when Timmy said, 'Aye Nurse. I saw him up the hill with a couple of soldiers.'

'Soldiers?'

'Aye.'

Isobel continued to digest this information while attending to her surgery duties, but once free and on her bike, she let her mind wander over the possibilities of what on earth Bobby was up to. He had no money to speak of and no friends that she knew of. He'd been gone overnight, had they arrested him and taken him off somewhere. If so, for what and to where?

That evening she was back in *The Apple*.

'I've seen more of you lately since that lad of the Lewises came back, but he's not in tonight.' Sylvia gave her a cheeky wink.

'He was seen being taken away by a couple of soldiers.'

'Who, Jack Lewis?'

'No, Bobby Dunn.'

'Oh him, why what does it matter?'

Isobel slumped down at the table in the far

corner of the snug. 'I don't know. I suppose I feel responsible for him.'

'Rubbish,' Sylvia snapped, fussing with a piece of binding that had come away from the neck edge of her dress.

'You don't suppose Jack could have anything to do with it, do you?'

Sylvia's attention came back to her friend. 'Why would Jack have anything to do with Bobby Dunn?'

'I don't know, except well, he did seem rather put out when he found Bobby living at the farm and being such a help to Duncan. Perhaps now he has found more help for his parents he doesn't want Bobby there any more.'

'Don't be silly. I'm sure he has far more important things to worry about than Bobby Dunn. The girls are helping out up at Pine Tree now,' Sylvia laughed. 'And by the look of it there is enough work going around to keep everyone busy. The girls are whacked; they hardly ate any dinner and collapsed onto their beds not long after. I don't think they are going to be as much trouble as I had anticipated.'

Isobel smiled knowingly. She was very fond of Sylvia, but she wouldn't find any answers here. No, she decided she would ask Jack straight out when she saw him tomorrow night.

*   *   *

Saturday night started out badly when Jack was late. Isobel had been ready for twenty minutes and walking up and down the living room working herself into a furious temper when she thought she was to be stood up yet again.

'Sorry I'm late. I phoned ahead and they have kindly agreed to hold our table. I'm glad you're ready.'

His effrontery took the words clean out of her hotly practised welcome.

Gritting her teeth she flounced past him in the doorway and down the path to the gate. The car with the same driver stood idling by the pavement. They climbed in and the car moved off.

'Where are we going?' her curiosity aroused now they were actually on the move.

'I thought we would go to a place in Rennington I'm rather fond of. Chap I met in the hospital introduced me to it. His brother owns it and Mary, his wife, does all the cooking. I think you will like them.'

The restaurant did not fail to delight her. Tucked away in the corner of the busy market town, the owners had managed to provide them with steak and garnish the like of which was unprecedented in wartime Britain.

The cosy but uncrowded atmosphere with its mural covered walls and soft Mediterranean decor of green shrubs and gingham tablecloths, bare wood floors and plain wood furniture allowed Isobel to relax.

Eric and Mary Keenlyside came out of their kitchen to meet them and Jack made the introductions. Eric was as thin as his wife was plump and as bald as his wife's long black tresses were thick, but both wore an engaging smile that encompassed their visitors in a warm and friendly welcome.

Isobel allowed Jack to order for her. As they munched their way through warm bread and a soft cheese and spinach dip while waiting for their meal they made small talk until Jack mentioned Bobby.

Immediately he had Isobel's full attention. 'What, what was that about Bobby Dunn?'

'I just mentioned what a fund of knowledge he has about the woods and moorland in and around the area.'

'Yes, well he would, having lived a large part of his life around these parts.'

He sat back looking relaxed as he wiped crumbs from his mouth with his serviette. 'I don't mean like you and I know the place. I mean his great knowledge of the local flora and fauna, the lie of the land and where things can be found and hidden. Does he talk to people about the wildlife and nature to be found around here? He is really interesting to listen to.'

Isobel thought for a moment then said, 'He doesn't like people in general so no, he doesn't talk about what he knows. I remember being amazed at how skilful he was when he lived in the woods just after he left the hospital. At first I was afraid he would starve, but then I saw him provide himself with rabbits and fish which he cooked in a basic but professional way. Yes, I suppose he does know more than people give him credit for.'

Then she sighed. 'In other ways he is very childlike with swift mood swings and temper tantrums. He can be extremely difficult which is why I'm so worried for him now he has gone missing.'

Their starter arrived with a cheerful, 'Bon Appetit' and they both tucked in.

When they had finished they laid down their cutlery and with a sharp look in her direction Jack said, 'He hasn't gone missing as such, he is scouting for a couple of my men who are looking for an escaped prisoner.'

Isobel felt her jaw drop open. 'What,' she gasped when she caught her breath.

A frown dropped between his brows. 'It's under wraps at the moment. No need to upset the locals and cause a panic if they should decide that they might be murdered in their beds.'

'Why, is this prisoner dangerous?'

'No, not at all, but you know what people are like once their imaginations take hold.'

'So where is he, when will he be back?'

Just then their steak arrived in a beautiful

cream, tomato, onion and basil sauce, and she had to wait for her answer as Jack bit into his dinner.

'He'll be back before you are, tucking into one of Mother's bran cakes if I'm not mistaken,' he said between bites. She looked up and caught him watching her with a gleam in his eye.

'What's funny?'

'You are with your need to mother all your chicks, yet you were ready to murder poor Mackenzie.'

'Yes well, that was different. He rubs me up the wrong way.'

'Then I can see I am going to have to be on my best behaviour.'

Isobel's heart gave a little skip and she choked on her last piece of cheese.

*   *   *

It was true. Bobby was back safe and well, having come to no harm from this excursion with the soldiers. Had they found the missing prisoner Isobel wondered, but refrained from asking, when she reminded herself that Jack had wanted it kept secret for fear of worrying the locals.

The Lewis family were just glad to have Bobby back and were happy with his, 'been to the woods,' explanation. Churchill dogged his every footstep, Joyce Lewis explained to

Isobel, and wouldn't let him out of his sight for a moment. 'So it's to be hoped he doesn't go walking in the woods again or he will have company the next time.'

Leaving the Lewis's farm Isobel had two more visits to fit in on the far side of the village. It was as she left the last house and was making her way back up the valley that she heard the baker's van rattling up behind her at a spanking pace.

Moving over to the side of the road she knew no more until she was knocked sideways into the ditch and watched the van disappearing up the road careering wildly from side to side behind the runaway horse.

When she tried to haul herself to her feet pain shot through her side making her feel sick. She laid still and quietly explored her body from her feet upward. There was a sickening pain in her left ankle but no obvious broken bones. The main pain was her side and she suspected broken ribs. Waves of pain made her eyes water.

She must have blacked out for the next thing she knew someone was lifting the bicycle back onto the road and asking her if she could stand. She gave a low groan and tried once more to drag herself out of the ditch.

This time with much grinding of teeth and the helping hand of the man holding the bike with one hand while reaching down to help her with the other, she managed to stand. Using the bike and the man for support they made it back to the village.

Between gasps for breath she told the man what had happened and asked him to enquire after the baker. He left her at the doctor's house and went to make the enquires. Doctor Turnbull burst into the kitchen where Mrs Holland was fussing around Isobel.

'What's to do here?' he said, shooing the housekeeper away.

Isobel repeated her story as best she could and said she thought she had broken her ribs. He examined her then strapped up her ankle and ribs, put her into his car and insisted that she went straight to bed when they arrived at the cottage.

'I will contact the nurse from down the valley and she can come and stay with you until you are fit again. Do as you are told, woman. You can't manage here on your own so that's an end to it.'

'But Nurse Thomson will have her own round to do. She won't have time to . . .'

'Well they will just have to arrange something else, now to bed with you.'

When he had gone Isobel hobbled into the kitchen to make herself a cup of tea then she sat down in the armchair in front of the fire with the blanket from Churchill's chair draped over her knees and let silent tears drop down her cheeks.

JACK SOFTENS TOWARDS ISOBEL

Bobby had helped them find the perfect sites for their work and Jack was well pleased. He had given up all hope of ever living a useful life again, when his friend Andrew Foreman gave him an introduction to a man in Whitehall.

Jack and the Major met in a tall wood-panelled room with a large oak desk and two straight backed chairs in the centre like an island in a sea of polished wood. The Major walked forward to shake Jack's hand, his grip had the firmness of a man who knows what he wants and how to get it.

The Major had suggested that Jack might be interested in using his skills as a serving officer to do some undercover work for a new department of the government. It would mean spending a couple of weeks training in the work that would be expected of him. Then he would be asked to take over a group of men in a secret operation that must on no account be discovered on pain of death.

Jack could hardly believe his good fortune. To be active again even in a small way was more than he had ever hoped for. After instruction he could see a way forward at last, and entered into the scheme with enthusiasm. Initially he was to take charge of a group of other officers based at the Hall where they were to set up a secret radio network. The old tramp had been invaluable in this endeavour and they now had six hidden dugouts arranged within an area around the camp.

*　　　*　　　*

It was two days before he heard the story of the runaway baker's van and realised that Isobel had been hurt. So that afternoon he paid a visit to her cottage. He knocked on the door several times without an answer and was about to leave when an upstairs window opened and Isobel's blonde head popped out.

'Oh hello, the door's open, just come in.'

He opened the door and stepped over the threshold.

'I'll be down in a moment, make yourself at home,' he heard her say before she came slowly down the stairs.

He looked about him at the dishes in the sink and the overburdened coathooks on the wall behind the door. A pile of laundry lay on a chair waiting to be ironed. A look of enquiry crossed his face as he made his way into the living room. They both entered the room at the same time.

'You'll have to excuse the mess. Nurse Thompson isn't the tidiest of people.'

He was shocked at how pale and fragile she looked and quickly made way for her to sit

107

down in the big armchair.

'I only heard about your accident this morning,' he said, sitting down opposite her. 'How are you?'

'Three cracked ribs and a twisted ankle. The bike has bent forks but the baker is all right. Apparently it was the crack of a shot gun that startled the horse, the baker fell back and banged his head and the horse bolted. I wouldn't have thought that horse had the energy to bolt, but you never know.'

She drew her breath in slowly after her little speech and grimaced.

He nodded. 'I'll get the bike repaired. How long will you be out of action?'

'Not long at all if I have any say in the matter. Sally Thompson has been very helpful, but she tires me out with her endless high spirits and disorganised chaos.'

'I was on my way up to the farm and I wondered if you would like a run up. The Land Army girls are up there now and making a big difference.'

He watched the colour creep back into her face and the grey eyes sparkle with sudden interest.

'That would be lovely, thanks. I haven't been able to get out and I'm going stir crazy.'

He led her out to the car that seemed always to be at his beck and call. The driver jumped out to hold open the door for her when he saw her strapped up ankle, and Jack helped her inside.

On the ride up to the farm Jack explained that his father hadn't been too impressed with Nurse Thompson. 'She's a little bit over the top if you get my meaning and that confuses Dad. I'm afraid you have spoilt them all. Mum has been asking after you, but Bobby said it served you right for cutting off Churchill's tail. I must confess that even I was confused with that one until Mum explained Churchill was the cat. Though why you cut his tail off I can't imagine, unless it was that Irish temper of yours getting the better of you again.'

Isobel stared at him in open-mouthed astonishment. 'I didn't do it deliberately. He had been mauled and it was hanging by a thread, it was the only thing I could do. Do you mean Bobby is holding a grudge against me, but I did try to explain to him why I had to do it.'

Jack was openly laughing at her. 'Calm down. I'm sure he will forgive you in time.'

Mischief made her say, 'Which one? Bobby or Churchill?'

'Both.'

Then the car stopped at the farm gate and the driver got out to open it.

'I will have to see if they will allow us to surface this lane up to the farm. Its condition worsens every year.'

'Can you do that?' she asked with interest.

'Well, it will take a gang of men over a

period of time, and then there will be the guarding of them, but I can always ask.'

'It will be great if you could,' she said with feeling, the thought of the nerve jangling ride up and down the lane to the farm still fresh in her mind.

'Oh, Nurse Ross how good to see you,' Joyce Lewis greeted her. 'Duncan has missed you. The other nurse is very nice of course, but he keeps on about you, wanting to know where you are.' She fussed around them as they entered the kitchen. The driver had followed them in at Jack's invitation.

'Mum, Dad, this is Wally Tennent my driver and right-hand man.' There was handshaking and lively chatter going on when Bobby came in not long after. Looking rather uncomfortable Wally turned away muttering something about seeing to the car. By the look of surprise on Bobby's face he had not only seen him but recognised him. Isobel noticed this and unconsciously frowned.

If Bobby looked so pleased to see him, why did the driver make such a hasty exit she wondered. Duncan was saying something to her and she turned her attention back to him. After an hour they were on the point of leaving when Isobel found herself standing next to Bobby.

'Has Churchill forgiven me, Bobby?'

Bobby nodded his head. 'Animals don't hold grudges, not like people.'

'Do you know Wally well?'

Again he nodded his head. 'Me and him meet in the woods. Find good places to hide.'

About to ask him more she was interrupted by Jack who was holding the door open for her. She looked hesitantly across at Wally but decided against asking him what he had been doing in the woods. Perhaps it had been a bit of illegal poaching that he didn't want known about, or perhaps it had something to do with the missing prisoner. She put it to the back of her mind when Jack asked if she had enjoyed her visit to the farm.

'I hope it wasn't too much like work.'

'Not at all. I look on your parents as friends. They are lovely people.'

He smiled down at her. 'Perhaps when you are more mobile we can repeat our trip into Rennington.'

Isobel tried to reply with practised equilibrium while her nervous system went into spasm. Their first meal had been just that, a drive into town, a meal with genial conversation and a drive back. No hint of anything else, yet here he was suggesting a second date. He was a man with hidden sorrows, she knew that, and would not look beyond the friendship he was offering, yet it was hard to check the fluttering in her stomach.

*   *   *

The day she returned to work was a day of soft warm winds and fluffy powder puff skies, so she left off her navy cardigan and set off on her recently restored bicycle. She had seen nothing of Jack since her trip up to the farm and assumed it was because he was busy.

In the days since she had frequently wondered whether anything would come of his offer of another date in Rennington, then scolded herself for caring about whether he did or not. This morning, however, she had placed Jack Lewis firmly to the back of her mind because Alan was coming home on leave.

She was too cautious to make plans, but the pleasure of her thoughts must have shown on her face for that morning everyone who knew her smiled and waved back as she passed. She and Alan would walk in the hills and take a picnic.

Alan loved to walk and they would lie in the grass as they had done when they were children staring up at the sky and make animals and magic people out of the clouds, as their mother did in the smoky embers of the fire of a winter's evening.

Later as teenagers they had spent their summer vacations walking and skiing in many different countries. Then their parents had died and life became a more serious affair. Alan had joined the RAF and she had completed her nursing training and taken the job here in Thornbury.

Her thoughts were brought back to the present by the sudden eruption onto the road in front of her of a small boy with a white scared face. Braking sharp enough to raise the rear wheel from the road, she asked the small boy what was wrong. With tears pouring down his face he managed to say, 'He's under the wagon.'

Swiftly dismounting from the bike she dropped it onto the verge and hurried after the boy who was running back towards a row of farm cottages a few yards up the track.

Never having had any calls to these particular cottages before she was horrified when turning into the yard behind them to notice the dilapidated state of the area. Her patient was trapped under the wheelbreak of a heavy wagon. Three women were trying to lift the weight from the man as a young boy tried to pull him out.

'Leave him,' she called out to the young boy, 'get something to prop it up with.'

Running up she placed her bag on a stone wall and bent down to the man lying groaning beneath the wagon. The women had failed to move it and let the wagon rest back on the man.

'Quickly,' she said, turning to the women. 'Help the boy gather something to push under the wagon the next time you lift it.' After only moments they were back with a number of items that Isobel accepted would make a support if a precarious one, and then once again the women gathered their combined strength and with a shout heaved the wagon upward. Isobel and the lad ran around shoving the things under the wagon to support it then the women let the weight go.

Grabbing the man under the armpits and digging in her heels Isobel tugged him slowly backward. He was heavy and the ground beneath them rough, but clamping her teeth tight she heaved him free of the wagon and the women let out a satisfied shudder.

The man was now unconscious. 'What's his name?' she asked the women standing alongside her.

'Ray.'

'Ray! Ray, can you hear me? A blanket if you please and we'll carry him inside.'

There was a slight hesitation and she glanced up at the two anxious work lined faces of the older women.

'He's not one of ours,' the grey haired woman said. 'He's a field worker.'

'Then where does he live?'

The women shrugged.

'Well he can't lie out here.'

One of the women disappeared into the nearest cottage and brought out a blanket which they used as a makeshift stretcher to carry the man inside. They laid him on a large bed in the far corner of the room. The place stank of damp and decay.

There was a fire in the grate around which were arranged a large black kettle and an equally large pot, a skillet and a wicked looking pair of tongs. The floor was packed earth with a greasy hooky mat before the fire. Green mould decorated the walls and the door and window frames barely met the holes they were designed for.

Isobel had retrieved her bag and moved to examine her patient. After a while she looked up and said, 'Someone will have to go for the doctor, this man is badly hurt. The boy can take my bike, it's outside by the road.'

As Isobel finished speaking one of the women turned and called out across the yard to the older lad, 'Freddie, the lady wants you to go to the village and fetch the doctor. You're to take her bike.'

The lad came forward scratching beneath his thatch of hair. 'I never ridden a bike afor,' he said.

'Well now's your chance,' Isobel snapped, 'and be quick, this man may need to go to hospital.'

The boy took off at a run and Isobel sat back to keep a watch on her patient.

When the boy came back he just shook his shoulders. 'The woman said the doctor was out on a case, she'll pass message on when he returns.'

Isobel frowned. 'Did she say where the emergency was?'

'No.'

'Then we must get this man to hospital,' she said as she wiped away the blood from the corner of his mouth. 'Boy, go back to the village, stop at the first telephone you see and dial nine, nine, nine and ask for the ambulance and tell them where you live.'

The boy set off once more at a run. A few minutes later he was back in the doorway. 'I thought I told you . . .' She got no further when a dark figure loomed in the doorway and nudged the boy to one side.

'Can we take him in my car? It will no doubt be quicker.'

Isobel looked up into the questioning face of Jack Lewis.

'Yes please, that will be most helpful,' she smiled gratefully.

Together they carried him carefully out to the waiting car and lay him on the back seat with his head resting on Isobel's knee.

*   *   *

The hospital was very busy and for a while she lost track of Jack. After handing over their patient he had made some excuse she had failed to pay attention to and disappeared. Now she fretted about getting home to her duties should he not return, but before she

116

could do anything she caught sight of him higher up the corridor talking to a doctor. Relieved she hurried towards them.

As she approached Jack said something to the doctor who turned, and casting an enquiring glance at her, held out his hand. 'Hello, my name is Drew Foreman. Pleased to meet you.'

Surprised at her warm welcome, Isobel shook hands. 'Isobel Ross.'

'We were just talking about you. Jack is an old friend of mine. He was just telling me what a good nurse you are.'

Isobel shot a surprised look at Jack who nodded in confirmation.

'Perhaps you and Jack could dine with my wife and I tonight.'

'Well, I should be getting back,' she hesitated.

'We would love to, Drew, but for now we must both be getting back to work.'

Andrew Foreman grinned. 'Of course, sorry. Make it eight o'clock.'

Jack nodded and they took their leave, Jack hustling her towards the main entrance.

'What did you mean by accepting that invitation? I didn't say I could go to someone's house for dinner.' She tugged herself free of his arm as they approached the car. Wally was leaning against the bonnet in the sunshine puffing on the last of his cigarette. He dropped the butt when he saw them coming and ground it out on the road with his heel before climbing into the car and taking his place behind the wheel.

'Are you working tonight?'

'No, but that's not the point. I have things to do. My brother is coming on leave shortly.'

'Good. I'd like to meet him.'

Isobel turned a shocked expression on him. 'Why?'

The car turned down onto the road and the sun through the window blinded her momentarily. As it shifted slowly across the back seat his face was in shadow. Was it her imagination or did he sound afraid, and if so of what?

The silence stretched on and eventually the car came to a stop at her gate and she was on the point of getting out when he said, 'I'll pick you up at seven-thirty,' and drove off before she could reply.

Someone had brought her bicycle back and parked it against the fence. So with a hearty sigh she mounted it and set off on her disrupted rounds. It was well into the afternoon before she returned to the cottage just in time to heat the water and have a cup of tea and a relaxing bath before getting ready for her dinner date at the Foremans' house.

Jack was on time as was she. He was quiet and thoughtful as they travelled back to Rennington. Surreptitiously she watched his face in the dwindling light. The high planes of

118

his cheekbones were still sharply defined, though the dark hair was thick and glossy now it still fell over his forehead.

He had large generous ears, a thing she always noticed about anyone, the shape of their ears, and long thin hands, artist's hands, she thought, as her glance dropped to where one hand rested on his stick handle, the other on his knee. He turned his head without warning and caught her gaze in his own.

'He's a pilot, your brother?' was all he said in reply to her earlier unanswered question

She nodded and a short while later they arrived.

A detached house in a row of houses running up a hill on the outskirts of the town. There was a short drive and a flight of four steps up to the front door. Drew and a beautiful woman a little older than herself stood at the open door to greet them. Drew introduced his wife as Barbara and they were led into the house. Drew took their coats while Barbara showed Wally into the kitchen then came back to escort Isobel into the lounge for drinks.

Later in the evening Isobel discovered that Drew was the doctor who had effected the change in Jack's life by introducing him to someone in authority in the south. Now they talked about conditions at the camp and the welfare of the POWs.

'No more work talk, please,' Barbara

119

interrupted them. 'Drew, let's have some music. Put the gramophone on and we can have requests. What's your favourite tune, Isobel, and we'll see if we have it.'

Drew crossed to the wind-up machine and began to sort through the records in the cabinet beneath.

'Vera Lynn?'

'OK, how about *The White Cliffs of Dover*? Barbara bought that one last week.'

'I brought it back from Newcastle. There has been some terrible bombing down by the docks. The friend I met in Fenwicks said there were great gaps in the rows of houses at the bottom of her street. Ambulances had come and taken the stricken families to other accommodation. We are getting a couple of evacuees next week. We have no children of our own,' she explained to Isobel. 'I just hope they don't give us little ones, with me not having any experience of children.'

'Oh I'm sure they won't.' Isobel smiled confidently.

The record had come to an end and Barbara suddenly said, 'Put some Mantovani on and let's dance.' She got up and joined her husband at the cabinet, there was some quiet bickering going on then the music from Ivor Novello's *Dancing Years* floated out across the room. Drew rolled up the carpet and walking over to where Isobel sat, bowed with a flourish and asked her to dance.

'But,' she said, glancing across to where Barbara was pulling Jack to his feet.

He grinned, 'Never met anyone yet who could refuse her anything.'

Together they waltzed gently around the room each couple taking care to avoid the other. When the record came to an end Drew put on another one and took hold of his wife leaving Jack and Isobel facing one another. Barbara leant her head to one side urging Isobel to take the lead. So Isobel stepped forward and placed a hand on Jack's shoulder.

She felt a shudder run through him so she placed her other hand in his and a bolt of emotion shot through her, then they were moving hesitantly one foot at a time.

After that the night flashed by and soon they were saying their goodbyes and climbing into the car again. The journey back was quiet but not with the stressed silences that they had arrived with, rather a tired, peaceful silence.

'Have you enjoyed yourself?' he asked when the car stopped at her gate.

'Immensely. Thank you.'

'Good,' he said, as he climbed out to escort her to the door of the cottage. 'Then perhaps we could make arrangements to go out again, say towards the end of the week?'

'Perhaps.'

They stood together for a while in silence then he said, 'Well goodnight then,' and walked up the path back to the car.

ISOBEL WONDERS ABOUT
JACK'S SECRET

Alan came home on leave two days later. She thought she saw more wrinkles around his tired eyes and there was definitely grey in his hair above his ears. Their banter had a flatness to it and eventually they stopped trying, and sitting in front of the fire talked quietly about everyday things like Churchill's shift of alliance and the patient she had found trapped under the cart and her subsequent dinner at the Foremans'.

'We,' he enquired, after she slipped up in her description of her meeting with Drew at the hospital.

'Jack Lewis, he gave us a lift to the hospital. Doctor Foreman is a friend of his.'

'So you weren't alone on this date?' He cocked an eyebrow at her.

With a soft laugh she replied, 'It wasn't like that. I haven't seen him since nor do I expect to.'

'Oh dear, when a woman says that, you know she is hoping for exactly the opposite.'

Throwing him a disdainful glance she rose from her chair and went into the kitchen to make them some tea.

He called after her, 'Where do I find this Jack Lewis?'

'Don't you dare,' she threatened. Then the kettle whistled.

*   *   *

The following morning was windy, but the sun was bright and hot and they set out to walk in the hills. With a flask in her pocket, a couple of sandwiches and a bar of homemade toffee, she felt they were well provided for. They had been walking for a couple of hours when Alan suddenly stopped and said, 'Listen.' Faint on the wind they heard what sounded like whispering in the tall trees, but as they waited amid the bleating of distant sheep they heard a cry of distress.

'Quickly! This way,' Alan said, hurrying off along a track that led them up onto a crag. Stopping every now and then to get his bearings they eventually looked down onto a rocky ledge where a figure sat with her back to the rock wall hugging an injured leg.

When Alan shouted down a tear-stained face of a young woman looked up.

'Oh, thank heaven! Please help me.'

'Are you alone?' Isobel called.

There came a lot of sobbing then with the shake of her head and in a weak voice she cried, 'No, my friend is down there.'

Alan swore. He turned to look at his sister, who whispered, 'What shall we do?'

He plunged hands deep into his jacket

123

pockets, a frown of concentration on his face. 'You will have to go for help. I'll try to get round to the foot of the crag and see what state the other one is in. You know these hills as well as I so it shouldn't take you too long. The girl will just have to wait it out.'

Isobel nodded. 'The only farms between here and the village are Lewis's and Hedley's. The Lewises have help but no telephone, but Hedley's is the farthest away.'

'Try the Lewis's farm, all we need is a stout rope and some blankets and someone to go to the village and fetch help.'

Isobel set off and Alan leant over the cliff to explain to the woman what was happening. Her hysterical cries for help followed Isobel for the next several minutes. She arrived at Pine Tree Farm puffing and panting. Ignoring the geese, she crossed the yard and dashed into the kitchen. The farmer, his wife and Bobby Dunn were just sitting down for their dinner and looked up in surprise at Isobel's unexpected arrival.

'There's been an accident on Dunster Crags, we need some help.'

Mrs Lewis was up from the table in a second. 'I'll call the girls. Bobby, away with you to the village and ask Mrs Holland to send help then find Jack and tell him there's been an accident.'

'I knows crags,' Bobby said, pushing his chair to one side. 'You stay put boss,' he said, patting Duncan's hand. 'I'll take Jack to crags, missus.'

'Good lad,' said Mrs Lewis on her way out the door.

In no time at all Isobel with the two girls, as the POW was not allowed to leave the farm, a length of rope and a couple of blankets, a make-do first aid kit and a flask of hot tea, were making their way back over the hills to the crags. When they arrived there was no sign of Alan. Isobel went to the edge of the cliff to peer down at the woman sitting there.

'Hello, help is here, we'll soon have you safe. What's your name?' There was no answer. She called repeatedly but there was no reply.

Alan called to them from way over to their right and a few moments later he appeared coming along the top of the crag towards them. 'The chap down below is dead now. He was dying when I reached him. I had to stay with him.' He tried to smile at her but his jaw was clenched tight.

'There's no response from below,' she said, as he set the girls to work tying the rope round an out-jutting boulder. Isobel tied one of the blankets into a makeshift sling before exploring her quickly-snatched first aid kit.

Alan was tying the far end of the rope around his waist when she looked up. Biting her lip she watched him carefully lower himself over the edge of the crag. She moved as far as she dared to the edge of the crag and called down to the woman. The rope tautened and Alan called back that she was unconscious.

'The ledge is quite wide so I'm taking my rope off. Pull it up and attach the sling and lower it down again.'

Take care, she prayed, signalling to the girls to pull the rope up. As she turned to attach the sling a truck roared up the track and bumped over the rough ground to come to a squealing stop only yards from where she stood. Three men jumped down from the open backed vehicle and pulled out ropes and a basket woven stretcher as well as props and a mallet to hammer them in with. Jack climbed down from the cab to co-ordinate the operation as the props were sunk and ropes attached to support the stretcher.

'My brother is down there on the ledge with the injured woman,' Isobel told them. 'I was about to throw this sling over the side.'

Jack walked to the edge and looking down called to Alan, 'I have a stretcher on supports. We'll send a sling down for you and when you are secure we'll send the stretcher down and you can steady her up.'

Isobel heard Alan answer then the blanket was secured to the end of the rope and lowered down for Alan to climb into. Now two of the men let the stretcher swing gently outward and once it had steadied began to

126

lower it gently to the ledge.

There were several calls up and down as Alan negotiated the woman into the stretcher. Between them the men then very slowly began to drag the stretcher upward. As they brought it over the edge Isobel could see that the woman was still unconscious. Then Alan appeared safe and well.

Isobel bent over the woman and went to work on a broken leg to give it temporary support, wrapped her in both the blankets and helped the men carry her on the stretcher into the back of the truck. Behind her Alan was telling Jack about the dead man at the bottom of the crag. She turned from the truck to join them.

'She needs to get to hospital right away. I've done all I can for her here.'

'Right, well, Wally will take you and the patient to hospital and drop the girls off at the farm on the way. The rest of us will stay here and retrieve the man from below then wait for the police.' Jack had taken charge of the situation but Isobel glanced at Alan for confirmation. He gave her a slight nod. 'You go ahead, I have to show them where the dead man is lying.'

Jack had turned back to his men as she walked back across to the truck and climbed in. It was a bumpy ride back to the farm where they dropped the girls and joined the road to the hospital.

127

Alan turned up in the doctor's car as Isobel was sitting in the corridor waiting for a lift back to the village. They had followed the police van in and the doctor was needed to attend the dead man's post mortem. Not long after that Jack arrived in the car driven by Wally.

'I wondered how you would get back,' he said as he walked up to them. 'And as I had business in town anyway I thought I might offer you a lift.' Alan grinned, 'Thanks, much appreciated.'

'I have a parcel to pick up here at the dispensary then we can be on our way.' As he walked off along the corridor Isobel cast a wary eye at her brother.

'You two seem very friendly?'

Alan glanced down at her. 'He's a handy chap to have around. Pushes himself to his limits but doesn't make the mistake of going over the top.'

She looked thoughtful for a while then said, 'Yes he's coping very well.'

'Quiet waters and all that, Sis. I wouldn't get too involved if I was you.'

She looked up startled, he sounded as though he meant it. Did she want to get involved, she wasn't sure. Something about the man attracted her, but what was it that tugged at her, making her heart miss a beat, catch her breath or even care. Not pity, nor the caring she gave to her patients, but something else,

128

something different. He had collected his parcel and was walking back towards them, his limp more pronounced than usual when it struck her, I think I love him.

The knowledge was such a surprise that she took a step back and bumped into Alan. 'Whoa,' he laughed steadying her by the shoulders.

'You should have gone out to the car,' Jack said, as he caught up to them. They walked out of the hospital together and joined Wally in the car. Isobel and her brother chatted amiably in the back of the car while all the time she was only too aware of the tall dark man sitting silently in the front beside Wally.

*　　　*　　　*

Alan's warning about Jack being the strong silent type, who would smother his fears rather than bring them out into the open and deal with them nagged at her long after he had gone back to his squadron. She saw such improvement in Jack that she was sure Alan was wrong.

After all, the war office would hardly have given him this job if they thought he was going to freeze every time there was an accident or lose his head in times of trouble. His behaviour at the clifftop had been exemplary in the way he had organised things once they had arrived. No, she thought, sinking her sore feet into a bowl of hot water, Alan is definitely wrong.

*　　　*　　　*

The doctor had been called out to Beacon Hill by Farmer Heron because his three children were unwell. The children had been diagnosed with scarlet fever and all three had been rushed into the fever hospital in Rennington. While the doctor had been called away Isobel had covered a local birth, her normal rounds, and Macky Mackenzie who'd had the misfortune to fall from his ladder while fixing guttering, and then back to the doctor's to do evening surgery. Now her feet ached and she was worn out.

She missed Churchill's ready welcome now he was no longer there to greet her and was deciding on the advisability of acquiring another pet when there was a knock on the door. Hissing blue murder to herself she stepped out of the bowl and made a quick dab with the towel. More rattling on the door and she shouted out that she was coming.

Hobbling over to the door she inched it open. 'Hello, what do you want?' The woman on the other side of the doorthresh looked vaguely familiar.

'My name is Ethel Feather. I work for Mr Heron and I think someone should come and see to him.'

Isobel frowned, her feet were getting cold. 'What's the matter with him?'

'He hasn't been himself since his wife died. The children have been taken into care and well, it's all been too much and he's storming around the house knocking things over and now he's cut himself and he won't let me help.'

Isobel counted to ten. 'The children aren't in care, they are in hospital because they have scarlet fever.'

'Yes, but everyone knows you die of scarlet fever.'

'Not any more, Mrs Feather. Mr Heron should go to the surgery if he has cut himself.'

'I don't know where that is. I only remembered where you were because of earlier visits when Mistress was alive. Besides, I can't be taking him anywhere now because he's flat out.'

With a heavy sigh Isobel turned back into the house. 'Wait there. I'll be with you in a moment.' She put on her stockings and pushed her sore feet back into her shoes then picking up her bag followed the woman out.

At the farm the first things they saw were the broken window and the chair lying in the garden. Ethel Feather led the way into the house, stepping carefully around the tipped-over hall stand. In the lounge items from the mantle piece, piano and bookcase had been swiped to the floor and lay in a broken mess. In another room papers had been pulled from

131

a cabinet and scattered. Heavy silver trophies knocked over and French windows stood open to the evening sky.

'He's out here, Nurse,' Ethel said as she made her way out into the garden.

Heron lay spread out across a flower bed and had bled profusely from a head wound which was now clotting.

Isobel bent over him to examine his head. 'The bleeding has stopped so I suggest you go down to the cottages and get some of the men to come up and move him to his bed.'

'Oh, but doesn't he need to go to hospital?'

Isobel sighed. 'No, he doesn't need hospital, he just needs to go to bed and sleep it off.'

'But what if he is no better when he wakes up?'

'Well, he'll have a terrible headache and he should come down to surgery and get that cut seen to.'

'Oh dear. I don't know what the poor Mistress would have done.'

About to leave, some instinct made Isobel turn back. 'Does Mr Heron get drunk often?'

'Oh no, it's his head you see. Mistress always knew what to do to calm him down.'

'What about his head?' Isobel wanted to know.

'Pain drives him mad. Mistress told me she knew what to do, but I thought I'd better . . .'

'Is the telephone still working?'

Looking startled the woman stared back at

132

the house. 'In the study.'

Making her way back into the house Isobel searched for and found the telephone and when she picked up the receiver was relieved to hear that it was working. She rang the doctor and told him what had occurred. Then gathering cushions and a tartan rug returned outside.

'Mr Heron will be going into hospital after all Mrs Feather. The doctor is on his way here now.'

*   *   *

At Pine Tree Farm on Tuesday morning she was telling Joyce Lewis about the Heron children and what a run of bad luck the family was having.

'He was lucky his housekeeper went to you for help. Why I don't know how we would have managed this past year without your help and kindness. Jack is always saying how generous and open hearted you are with everyone.'

'Is he,' Isobel murmured as she bent to undress Duncan's leg.

Joyce went on talking but it all floated over Isobel's head, for inside her heart was echoing between her ribs. She would give anything to know exactly what it was that Jack thought about her. Then Duncan looked down with a grin on his face and said, 'You and our Jack would do well together, Nurse.'

133

She felt the blood rush to her face and in a voice slightly higher than normal said, 'Duncan Lewis, you just keep your ideas to yourself.'

He chuckled and winked at his wife.

Isobel washed her hands and left, turning down the usual cup of tea and chatter. As she steered her bicycle down the rutted track that Jack had promised to get resurfaced and failed, she called herself all sorts of a fool. He had never suggested another date on the few occasions when she had seen him and she had schooled herself into believing that he wasn't interested.

That didn't stop her from wondering about him and toying over Alan's suggestion that, like an iceberg, there was more beneath the surface than appeared above. What was it that Alan had sensed in Jack that she, as a nurse, should know but had missed?

By the time she reached the cottage and found Macky hovering by the gate she had closed off these thoughts.

'I need my arm seeing to, Nurse. The wrapping you put on is coming off, look,' and he offered his arm for her inspection.

'I'm off duty, Macky, you should attend the surgery tonight.'

'But it's my darts match the night, I can't be missing that.'

'And I have a pile of washing waiting to be done,' she snapped at him impatiently. It was unlike her she knew, to turn her back on anyone needing help day or night, on or off duty, but something about Macky's attitude, that she could be called on whenever it suited him, rattled her.

Slamming back the gate she pushed the bike down the path and when she looked back he was walking off down the road. She bit her lip shook her head and went into the house.

'You did right, girl. We can't be expected to be at their beck and call all hours of the day and night,' Doctor Turnbull said.

Which Isobel thought sounded ironic coming from the man who could be called out any time of the day or night in an emergency. Though heaven help anyone who called him out unnecessarily. She had mentioned the incident of Macky and the loose bandage because she was feeling guilty about the way that she had sent him off.

'The problem is he doesn't seem to be in the surgery and his arm really should be re-bandaged.'

'Then I dare say someone has done it for him and he has gone off to the darts match after all.'

Isobel went to call on the next patient and dismissed Macky and his bandage from her mind.

*　　　*　　　*

On Thursday morning she cycled up to the

lodge of Hotspur Hall. It was a lovely old house with a covered porch and a deep studded door. The nearest ground floor window was open to the early summer sun and as Isobel parked her bike she overheard voices arguing.

Not wanting to interrupt she considered withdrawing and coming back later but before she could make up her mind the door shot open and Sylvia's young cousin, Brenda, ran out nearly knocking Isobel off her feet.

She was quickly followed by an agitated Mrs Crombie who with a cloud of ruffled hair and two very pink cheeks came to a sudden stop in front of Isobel.

'Oh excuse me, Nurse. What can I do for you?' she asked Isobel while her eyes followed the disappearing Land Army girl.

'Perhaps I should come back later,' Isobel suggested.

'No no, come along in, come in,' she said, ushering her down the hall and into a beautiful sitting room.

'Was that Brenda Douglas that nearly knocked me down? I thought she would have been up at the farm.'

'Quite right, that is where she ought to be. But you know what these gals are like, Nurse, and when one is responsible for them well one must reprimand them on occasion.'

Poor Sylvia, Isobel thought, what on earth had the girl been up to. Leaving the subject well alone she put her request on behalf of the Heron children to the magistrate.

'With their mother dead and their father in hospital what will happen when the children come out of the fever hospital? The housekeeper at the farm tells me she can't stay with them and the foreman and his wife have four children of their own to care for.'

'Ah yes, poor Mr Heron. How is he doing, Nurse?'

'As well as can be expected, but Doctor Turnbull tells me it will be some time before he will be home again.'

'The children, of course, well we shall see what can be done. I have my hands full with the evacuees at the moment but perhaps I can find someone to take them in for a short time.'

Mrs Crombie sat back with a small frown between her brows. 'If not, then they will have to go into the Children's Home in Pennington.'

Isobel sighed. 'That would be a shame.'

'I quite agree, but unfortunately that is what it may come to and even then they may be sent onward. One just does not know these days.'

'I'll ask around my patients; see if anyone can help.'

'How old are the children?'

'Eight, six and four, I believe. A boy and two girls. They are still very distressed by the loss of their mother and would benefit greatly if they could be found somewhere where they could all be together if possible.'

'We will try our best, Nurse, it is the least we can do. What progress are they making in hospital?'

Isobel smiled. 'The doctor says it was a mild fever and they should be out in the next ten to fourteen days.'

Mrs Crombie rose to her feet and patting her hair back into place led Isobel from the room. 'Please let me know as soon as you're aware of the date of their release.'

'I will. Thank you.'

'Don't mention it, my dear.'

*   *   *

In Rennington the following day for a talk by the Medical Officer of Health at the local library, Isobel was passing the park on her way back to the bus stop when she noticed Barbara Foreman watching some children playing by the river. The next bus wasn't due for another hour so she made her way over to where the doctor's wife was sitting.

'Hello. Lovely day, isn't it.'

The other woman looked up and smiled. 'Isobel, isn't it?'

'May I join you?'

'Please do. The two little girls by the fence are our evacuees. I thought perhaps if I brought them down here after school they might find it easier to make friends. Their teacher says they make no effort to mix at

138

school. But as you can see it doesn't seem to be working.'

'It's early days yet,' Isobel said, in a soothing way.

'Of course. Andrew is always telling me I am too impatient. I want everything to happen now.' She gave a soft laugh and turned to Isobel on the seat beside her. 'But how are you? We haven't seen anything of you since you came to dinner. Nor Jack either, are you still seeing him?'

'We aren't a couple, I just happened to be there when your husband asked us to dinner.'

Barbara raised her eyebrows and gave her a questioning look. 'Andrew and Jack go back a long way and he swears Jack is interested. I know Jack can be a bit withdrawn, but he's had a bad time which has made him even more so, however I would have thought as a nurse, you might be prepared to understand that and give him a bit of leeway.'

Isobel watched a little boy make a tentative attempt to include the girls at the fence in his game by tossing a ball towards them. One of the girls ignored him but the other picked up the ball and threw it back. The two women saw this and smiled at one another.

'Jack has never shown me anything other than friendship and I value that, and as a nurse, yes, I understand how his injuries may have affected his outlook, but I don't see how I can do more to encourage him.'

'Do you want to?'

Isobel didn't answer for a long time. 'I don't know, perhaps, there is something that makes me want to know him better.'

'That will do for now,' Barbara smiled. 'When is your next day off?'

'It's supposed to be Wednesday if I'm not called out on an emergency.'

'Well, stick a note on your door and I will get Jack to pick you up and bring you over to us. It's our anniversary this weekend, but we will put off the celebrations until Wednesday when you can join us.'

'Please there's no need . . .'

'No need at all, but you'll come, won't you? About two we can eat in the garden and Andrew's uncle has promised us a surface for dancing.'

'Barbara, do you know how your husband persuaded Jack that he should go back to work?'

Barbara withdrew suddenly as though the question had taken her by surprise. Then a shadow crossed her face and she said, 'No, I'm afraid not.'

'When he first came home, he asked Duncan to help him die, did you know?'

Barbara gaze dropped to the ground and she said quietly, 'Andrew said he was depressed.'

'Then suddenly he was well again.'

'He needed a reason to live.'

140

'Pen pushing in charge of a POW camp,' Isobel shook her head, 'I don't see it.'

'As long as it worked.' Barbara said with a shrug.

Isobel glanced at her watch. 'I have to catch my bus now. Thank you for the invitation on Wednesday, I'll see you then.' And with a wave of her hand she hurried away as Barbara turned and called to the children.

Sitting on the bus as it made its way back to Thornbury, Isobel pondered on all Barbara had said or not said. Alan was right, there was something she wasn't being told.

The desperately depressed Jack she had first met was not going to be suddenly given a new lease of life because of a desk job, there was more to it than that and the fact that she was not considered suitable to be trusted with this information hurt her more than Jack's disinterest ever could.

People came to her with all kinds of problems, drawn not just by the uniform but because, as she liked to believe, they trusted her. From marital differences to advice about truancy, from the care of new babies to the signing of wills, and the feeling that the Foremans were keeping something about Jack's past from her gave her a sick feeling in her stomach.

Surely, she thought, it was natural to want to know everything about someone you were attracted to. You only had to look around to

141

see young girls rushing into marriage with virtual strangers before their men went off to war. What was going to happen when they returned and found they hardly knew one another.

The bus came to a groaning halt and Isobel climbed down. As she hurried home she passed the Post Office which was really just the front room of the owner's cottage. The two spinster sisters who ran it had their faces pressed to the window watching her go by.

An old man in the allotments stopped what he was doing and looked up as she passed. A woman with a shopping bag had stopped to gossip with an old lady sitting on a chair by her front door. They stopped their chatter to turn and watch the nurse go on up the street.

Isobel noting all the attention smiled to herself. The nosiness of her neighbours at times irritated her and the speed of the gossip astounded her. But on the whole it was harmless and well meant. She knew they would be dying to know where she had been and what she had been up to. As if I ever get the chance to get up to anything, she thought.

DREADFUL NEWS FOR ISOBEL

It was lying on the mat inside the door. It didn't register at first and she almost missed it,

142

stepping over it to take off her jacket and place her bag on the bench top. When she turned back her heart nearly stopped.

Small, thin and yellow with HMS stamped in the corner. The telegram everyone dreaded stared up at her as though daring her to pick it up. Squatting down she reached out unable to touch it for fear it would prove real, until with shaking fingers she closed them over it and walking through into the living room sat down heavily in the old chair.

Time shrank into nothingness; dying coals fell unheeded into the grate. The room grew dark and she hid in its darkness. She didn't dare to think, for if she did she would also feel and that would bring a pain she couldn't bear. Shivering she got to her feet, rebuilt the fire and automatically drew the blackout curtains. Tears coated her eyes but failed to fall as if by withholding them she could stem the inevitable. The band around her chest tightened until she could only breathe in little gasps. Then she had to get up and be sick.

Later she crept back to the chair ignoring the telegram by the hearth. She woke at four in the morning and opened the telegram. It stated that her brother's plane had been hit by enemy fire over the North Sea and the loss of life noted. Tears came in great wracking sobs until finally she climbed wearily up to bed.

*   *   *

143

By morning the doctor too had heard the gossip and he grieved for the nurse he had grown so fond of. When Mrs Holland had told him with tears in her eyes, he had bowed his head and shaken it slowly from side to side. He'd patted her shoulder and grunted something unintelligible and taken himself off to his surgery.

Isobel arrived as usual fifteen minutes before surgery was due to open. One look at her face and the doctor muttered something into his chest and concentrated on the paper work in front of him on the desk. Patients arrived, were seen to, and departed. When the last one had gone the doctor leant back against his desk and stared from under bushy brows at the back of the girl tidying the trolley in front of her.

'Because we care for other people's suffering it doesn't make us immune against our own. I've added two more to your list for home visits. Work girl, that's the only answer,' he added gruffly.

Isobel nodded without turning around and finished what she was doing. Then taking down the woollen navy jacket she had put on earlier, not because the weather had grown colder but because she was having difficulty getting warm, she pulled it around herself and stuffed the extended list into her bag.

Passing the housekeeper on the way out she

was engulfed in a warm squashy embrace that smelt of lavender polish and cooking apples. Tears rolled freely down the woman's cheeks and Isobel biting her lips pushed past her out of the door.

No smiles and happy waves greeted her this morning as she made her way through her list of visits, only solemn faces and sympathetic glances. In outward appearances nothing had changed. She chatted to her patients, enquired after the families and dished out advice and encouragement.

Today was her day for visiting Pine Tree Farm. When she arrived at the bottom of the track up to the farm there were men working on its surface, and because it was impossible to ride up she left her bike at the bottom and walked up. She was exhausted when she reached the gate and had to call several times before Joyce Lewis came hurrying to her rescue.

Once inside the house Duncan was waiting for her. They went through into the other room where she saw him through his exercises and dressed his leg before returning to the kitchen. There was a lot of chatter in the kitchen as the girls and the Polish helper had come in for their morning break.

Isobel was on the point of making a swift get away when Bobby surprised her in the doorway.

'Man who burnt Bobby's house down said

you will go away now your brother is dead.'

Isobel stared at the innocent concerned face before her. Shaking her head she said, 'I'm not going away, Bobby.'

'Bobby's glad,' he said, nodding his head vigorously.

She gave him a sad smile then turned away, but before she could stop herself she turned back and asked, 'Does the man who told you that have a name?'

Looking momentarily confused he shook his head, then enlightenment suddenly lit up his face and he said, 'Matty, bad man, Bobby doesn't like.'

'Do you mean Macky?'

Bobby nodded, 'Bad man.'

Isobel's lips were pressed tight together as she continued down the track and retrieved her bicycle.

*   *   *

The young man had been asked by Alan to deliver the letter should anything happen to him. And two days later he did. Isobel accepted it silently and didn't even ask the young man in. What could Alan possibly have to say to her now when it was too late. She picked up the poker and gave the fire a vicious jab. Then sank back and hugged the pain in her stomach. It was all far too late.

Her suffering had turned inward, torturing

her with memories of the past with what might have been in the future when this dreadful war was over. Resentment and anger fought with the loss and the loneliness. The letter lay in her lap and she stared through unshed tears at her name in his old familiar scribble before slowly prising it open and spreading out the single sheet.

Dear Sis
Don't shoot the messenger, it's the worst job in the world, but Craig has kindly agreed to deliver this for me. The missions are becoming more demanding and I fear this next one may be my last. I am sorry I couldn't have stayed around long enough to see you settled with your own home and family, but there is a little money in the bank to help see you through.

Please don't fret, walk up into the hills and I'll be there with the golden eagle as he rides the currents, and the deer as they graze the wild grass, in the song of the lark and the call of the grouse, and some day, God willing, you will come with others to laugh and play as we did.

Your ever loving brother
Alan

The next day she came home from her rounds to find Jack Lewis standing on her doorstep. 'I've only just heard about your brother.'

'The whole village has known for three days,' she said, wearily as she passed him to open the door.

'I'm only just back after a week down south.' He followed her into the kitchen, where she filled the kettle and, lighting the gas ring, placed the kettle on to it. He had moved on into the living room and was bending over Alan's open letter where she had left it on the chair seat when she had gone to bed last night. She came in quietly behind him and he swung round on his stiff leg to look down at her. They stood for several moments in silence then he opened his arms and enfolded her.

His jerkin felt rough against her wet cheek, though she was unaware of crying. To be held so close, and feeling so safe made her loss that much harder to bear. Sadly she pulled back as his finger wiped at a tear as it dribbled from her jaw.

He led her back to the chair where he picked up the letter before seating her down then sitting himself opposite. 'Will you do as he asked and walk in the hills?'

'Yes.'

He was sitting forward with his hands between his knees. His dark hair had fallen over his eyes and he swiped it back with his hand as he moved his position and leant back in his seat. With an empty expression and heavy lidded eyes it looked for all the world as

148

though he had fallen asleep but then he looked across at her and asked softly, 'Will you go alone?'

'Yes.'

'My parents send their love. They were unaware until Bobby told them.'

He stayed until it was time for her to go to evening surgery. As they parted company at the doctor's house before he went on to *The Apple* he said, 'I'll be back tomorrow.'

All her patients had offered heartfelt sympathy on her loss. Joyce Lewis always had some little home baked treat for her to take home with her and Jack visited most days. Doctor Turnbull while still gruff was kindly in the days following Alan's death though he kept her work load full to capacity.

Sylvia had been along to the cottage on several occasions but while Isobel was grateful for her friendship it didn't bring her the peace that Jack's company did. Towards the end of the summer when other people's losses had taken over the attention and the war news was worsening by the day Isobel began to realise just how dependent she had become on Jack's visits.

She still found herself watching for Alan's tall figure whenever she saw a bus disgorging its passengers at the village bus stop, glancing hopefully at any mail that popped through the letterbox, even though she knew it was never going to happen.

Was Jack Lewis really replacing Alan in her desperate need for someone to call her own, she asked herself one wet afternoon not long after he had left. He'd brought her a kitten from the farm and she felt its tiny claws as it kneaded the skirt in her lap. Picking it up she brought it level with her face. It was coloured very like Churchill with his same round face. It protested loudly at being inspected this way and with a soft smile she cuddled him close.

*　　*　　*

On the first of September Mrs Crombie knocked on her door. Surprised that she should come calling, Isobel invited her in and she stood in the centre of the living room like a galleon in a wrecker's yard. 'I have bad news regarding the Heron children,' she said before Isobel had a chance to offer her a seat.

'The couple I had left them with are elderly and have now decided that they cannot cope with such young and demanding children. I'm at the end of my tether and I'm afraid they will have to be turned over to the orphanage authorities.'

'But that could mean them being sent away to goodness knows where. Has anyone contacted Mr Heron?'

'That will be my next job of course, but I believe the poor man is to have brain surgery and it is doubtful even if the operation is a success that he will ever be in a position to care for his children.'

Isobel shook her head. 'Everyone I asked has already been approached to take evacuees, but I'll keep on asking. How long do we have before they have to be rehoused?'

Mrs Crombie's double chin quivered. 'I promised to look into it as soon as I could.' Loose tendrils had escaped her grey hair roll and the black hat atop her head tilted as she sank into the old armchair. Raising a hand to her head she adjusted the hat before saying, 'A few days at the most, I'm afraid.'

They sat in gloomy silence for a moment or two then Mrs Crombie said, 'Reverend Meeker has a family from London staying with him. They were bombed out a few weeks ago and the church sent them up here. They are a couple and their teenage daughter. Knowing how good the vicar's wife is with young children it seems a shame that they only have the one gal.'

In quiet contemplation she continued, 'The vicarage rooms are so large, a pity that one gal should have one all to herself. If it had only been the couple for example then I'm sure Daisy Meeker would have loved to have all three children.'

Isobel agreed with her, not seeing the trap she was heading into until the magistrate pounced. 'You have been so concerned about the welfare of these children, Nurse, I wonder if you could help me here. Could you possibly take in one well-behaved young woman? She would be company for you and I'm sure no bother at all.'

Isobel was shaking her head and on the point of saying that the room was Alan's when it hit her, that Alan would no longer have need of his room.

Mrs Crombie seeing Isobel's white face immediately retracted her request, 'Oh, my dear, I am so sorry, that was extremely tactless of me. Please forgive me,' she said, rising to her feet.

'If you will give me some time I will think about it.'

'Of course, my dear,' Mrs Crombie said, patting Isobel's shoulder.

Isobel saw her to the door then turned back into the room fighting the tears that threatened.

ACCUSATIONS ARE THROWN ABOUT

'You look tired nurse,' Joyce Lewis remarked one Friday afternoon when she arrived to shoo the geese away from the gate.

'The track is much better now it has been surfaced.'

'Oh yes, Duncan is thrilled to bits with it. Insisted on driving the horse and cart up and down himself the other day. Jack's here, said he wanted a word with you when you arrived.'

The geese were very bold that morning and attempted to attack both women as they crossed the yard. With a brandishing of her broom Joyce scattered them and Isobel passed safely into the kitchen. Bobby was sitting stuffing himself at the table while Duncan and Jack were talking by the fire. The men turned and smiled at her as she came in and placed her bag on the bench.

Bobby shuffled back from the table and getting to his feet moved across to where Duncan was sitting. 'Nurse wants you,' he said, indicating that Duncan should get up and follow him. Duncan laughed and allowing Bobby to take him by the arm went with him out of the room and down the passage.

Isobel nodded to Jack on her way past him and followed the two men to the room where Duncan received his treatment and exercises. When they came back into the kitchen some thirty minutes later Jack was waiting for her. She washed her hands and accepted Joyce's offer of a cup of tea and a bite to eat and was ready to leave when Jack got to his feet and offered to see her out.

'I called yesterday but you appeared to have company,' he said once they were out of earshot of the house.

They stopped at the gate and looking around Isobel asked, 'Where's the car?'

153

'Wally's coming back to pick me up later.'

'Yes, Mrs Crombie thought I should have some company now that Alan . . .' she couldn't continue.

He was frowning when she looked up at him. 'I see. I'll miss our talks.'

She dropped her head. So will I, she thought. 'The kitten is settling in nicely.'

'Good.'

There was an awkward silence then the geese came flying around the corner of the byre and across the yard towards them. Isobel quickly scrambled to the other side of the gate and Jack laughed.

Isobel stared at the change in his expression. Gone were the permanent tucks above his nose, his mouth was lifted in one corner showing a long dimple in his good cheek and the sadness that frequently clouded his dark eyes was for those few moments lit with humour. Her heart turned over in her chest and the need to tell him how she felt became a physical pain.

'Then perhaps you could let me take you to dinner again in Rennington one night.'

'I'd like that, thank you. I'm free this weekend.'

'Then I'll pick you up tomorrow night at eight and perhaps you can tell me the story of your visitor.'

She heard him scattering the geese as she cycled away down the road.

*   *   *

On Saturday evening she bit her lip and twisted this way and that before the speckled mirror in her bedroom. Was the blue dress too plain or would the red jumper and skirt look better? The kitten was kneading her bedspread and making funny hissing noises. She smiled at him and wished he could tell her what best to wear. It was so important to her that she made a good impression.

There had been such a fuss when she had insisted on having the first bath of the evening for there was never sufficient hot water left to provide a good second tub. Phyllis Barton, her new lodger, had taken to grabbing the first bath before Isobel was home from surgery, leaving her hostess to manage as best she could with what was left of the water.

Phyllis had only been at the cottage a few days yet already it felt like a lifetime to Isobel. The girl was very demanding and if ever Isobel looked as though she was about to object Phyllis would simply sigh and make out that perhaps she would have been better off staying at the vicarage.

Tonight Isobel had put her foot down and Phyllis was sulking before the fire as Isobel dressed for her date with Jack. Grey eyes glinted back at her from the minor's reflection as rain spattered on the window pane. The blue dress, her mother's sapphire and pearl brooch and the cream swing coat that had seen better days but was impossible to replace because of all the coupons it would take. Phyllis had brought her ration book but with many of the coupons missing and she couldn't or wouldn't say why.

It was nearly time, so dressing quickly she ran a brush through her hair and applied a little lipstick before hurrying down the stairs. The kitten followed her down the stairs, dashed across the floor and jumping at Phyllis's skirt clung fast. Phyllis, in a bad mood to start with, pulled the kitten from her skirt and flung it across the hearth where it picked itself up, shook itself and curled up on the rug in front of the fire. Isobel's face pulled into a disapproving frown. But she said nothing and then Jack was at the door.

*   *   *

'Well,' Jack said when they had finished their meal and were sitting with their coffee. 'Who is this girl that has been foisted onto you?'

Isobel replaced her cup into its saucer and staring across at Jack related the story of Phyllis's arrival.

'And is she good company?'

Isobel shrugged and looked away. 'I suppose so but . . .' Her voice caught in her throat.

156

'It's only natural that you still miss him.'

She looked at him then her eyes filled with confusion. 'I miss him because he's away, but I can't and won't believe he is dead.' She made a dismissive gesture. 'I would know if he were dead, Jack, because part of me would have died also.'

He was watching the coffee as he swirled his cup. 'Death is fickle. It can swallow up and spit out at will. If you want to hang onto hope then who is to deny you.' He put down his cup and reaching across the table covered her hand with his own.

On their return to the cottage Jack stepped down from the car to walk her up the path to her door. They said little on the doorstep then slowly Jack took her in his arms.

Isobel had just raised her face for his kiss when the door was flung open with a crash and a distraught Phyllis stood framed in the light from the kitchen.

'Where've you been? The chimney's smoking. I tried to open the door to let the smoke out and a nasty little man told me I had to close it,' she cried. 'I nearly choked to death.'

Jack had taken a step back at this intrusion and now he snapped, 'Get the door shut, you're displaying light.'

'Sorry, thank you for dinner,' Isobel cried as she pushed Phyllis back into the kitchen and following her slammed the door.

157

Mrs Crombie was greatly relieved when Isobel stopped her in the street one day to say that Mr Heron had come through his operation very well and was making excellent progress.

'That is wonderful news, Nurse. How is the Barton girl fitting in, not too much bother I hope?'

'She has given up her part-time delivery work at MacKenzie's, and point blank refuses to do anything to help with the war work. Her parents are paying for her keep but I don't know how I am expected to cope with her sitting around all day long.'

'Carry on, Nurse, as we all must do in these troubled times.' And she heft her large rear onto the bicycle seat and peddled off.

On Isobel's arrival at the surgery, Doctor Turnbull's first comments were about the sudden appearance of the new people at Beacon Hill. 'There are eleven in the family, the parents and nine children, all boys. The mother came down here to register them, said they didn't expect to need me for they were all healthy.'

Isobel smiled and said a silent prayer that it was so. 'Do you know what they will do with Mr Heron's things? Presumably they will have been packed up for him if these other people have already moved in.'

'Hmm, one would imagine so. I see they have managed to palm the Heron children off on the vicar and moved the Barton girl over to you, how do you feel about that?'

'There wasn't an alternative, Doctor. It was that or the Heron children being sent to the orphanage and I couldn't let them go there, not while there was the slimmest chance that Mr Heron might have time to organise some other future for them.'

The doctor was nodding his head absentmindedly as he rifled through some papers. 'Taking the world on your shoulders again, Nurse? I hope that girl is helping you out.'

* * *

Isobel was at the farm waiting for Bobby and Duncan to come in from the fields and Joyce from the dairy.

'I don't know how to thank you,' she said to Jack. 'I had no idea what I was going to do with her.'

When there was still no response from Jack she looked back over her shoulder at him. 'Is something wrong?' she asked quietly.

She knew he was a man of few words and hadn't really expected him to come up with an answer to her problem of what to do with Phyllis, so when he offered her a job at the camp she had been overflowing with gratitude,

159

but now she sensed his distance and it caused her concern. 'Jack?'

'There are no thanks necessary,' he said coldly.

'What's wrong?' She went to put an arm on his sleeve but he moved out of her reach.

Bobby and Duncan entered the kitchen and Isobel sighed. Duncan had reached what medical science considered was the limit of his potential recuperation since the accident and this was obviously not to Jack's liking. He wanted his father returned to the man he had been and this Isobel had warned him repeatedly, was always doubtful.

He didn't seem to understand how lucky Duncan had been and how grateful his mother was just to have her husband back with them again. That Duncan was more overseer than hands-on these days wasn't so important now they had the help they needed. But it seemed Jack wasn't satisfied, and Isobel had a horrible feeling he was blaming her.

Usually when she left the farm Jack would accompany her to the gate. But today he made the excuse he had to talk to his father, so Bobby came instead to check that the geese were nowhere in sight.

Isobel was full of warring emotions as she rode the now smooth path down to the road. They had been out twice more to the restaurant in Rennington and once to the Foremans' for Barbara's birthday party. Other than that the only place they met was on Isobel's visits to the farm when Jack would make the effort to be there at the same time.

That night she went along to *The Apple* to see Sylvia. No sooner was she in the door than Sylvia said, 'Norman had a blazing row with your fella last night. Nearly came to blows they did. I had to get some of the lads to help bundle Norm into the back.'

Isobel stared back at her friend. 'Do you mean, Jack?'

'How many fellas have you got?'

'I've told you he's not my fella, he's just a friend. Why on earth did he fall out with Norman?' Isobel's brows pulled down in a frown.

'Heaven only knows,' Sylvia shrugged, 'you know what men are like, pick a fight with their own shadows they will, though I must say I didn't think Jack Lewis was the type.'

'What was it about?'

Her friend became all agitated, then with a great sigh slumped over the bar and said quietly, 'I wish she'd never come.'

'Who?'

'Our Brenda picked up some talk from among the girls and repeated it to our Norm didn't she, well you know Norman, couldn't keep it to himself could he, had to repeat it in the bar. Your fella overheard your name being mentioned and that was it, he grabbed my Norm by the collar and nearly choked the life

161

out of him, I wouldn't have said he had the strength.

'What was it she said?'

'She said you were two-timing your fella with the Polish worker at the farm.'

Isobel was stunned. 'Why would she say a thing like that?'

'It's just gossip. We all know what these young girls are like, what they don't know, they make up. I've caught her on more than one occasion prancing about in her underwear in front of Norm and I've asked her time and again not to do it. Now I've had old Crombie ticking me off about her skiving off work. But the other night the Polish POW had told the girls that officers at the camp turned a blind eye to the prisoners meeting girls in the woods.' Her mouth took on a hard line then she burst out, 'She's more trouble than she's worth to me,' she added meaningfully.

When Isobel caught her meaning it was all she could do not to burst out laughing. What on earth did Sylvia think a young girl like Brenda would find attractive about a greasy-haired old leech like Norman. Suddenly she felt very sorry for her friend.

'Surely not, with all these handsome young servicemen around. I don't mean to be rude, Sylvia, but Norman is twice her age.'

'Oh I know, but she's such a flirt. The other girl is no bother at all. I hardly know she's there,' she said, turning to face the two men who had just come into the bar.

When Isobel caught sight of Macky she remembered Bobby telling her what Macky had said when Alan had died. 'I see your arm is better now,' she addressed him.

'No thanks to you,' he grouched.

'Perhaps, but then I don't go around telling people you've got rid of me just because I lost my brother.'

'What?' The man who had entered the pub with him stepped back in surprise. 'You never said that did you, Mac?'

Macky Mackenzie had gone a sickly shade of grey and he stared at her with anger in his eyes. His mouth quivered as he opened it to deny what she had said, but then he turned his back on her and said, 'I only told that old dolt, Bobby Dunn. It'll be him spreading the rumours around.'

The other men in the bar had turned to stare at them and Isobel, with a goodnight to Sylvia, left. She couldn't help but wonder why Jack had jumped to her defence in the bar when he had been so cold to her at the farm.

*　　*　　*

He was standing by the car waiting for her when she returned home.

'Jack?'

'Is the girl at home?'

Isobel shivered at his tone of voice. 'No,

she's out with friends.'

'Then could I have five minutes of your time?' It was more of an order than a request.

With a slight lift of her brows Isobel led the way into the cottage. In the living room he spun round to face her. 'How dare you gossip about me to all and sundry? It is imperative that my job at the Hall is kept low key yet now I hear you are asking questions about my work there.'

Whatever Isobel had been expecting it wasn't this furious tirade. The shock sent her backwards into the chair.

She bounced up again and standing toe to toe with him lifted her chin as she announced. 'I don't gossip.'

Dark blue eyes stared down into grey ones. 'Do you deny that you have been questioning Bobby Dunn about his relationship with Wally, or that you asked Barbara Foreman about me?'

Isobel screwed her face up as she thought back. 'No I don't deny it, but I wasn't gossiping.'

'Perhaps, but your nosing into my affairs gave rise to gossip and I may lose a very important job.'

'Well I'm very sorry to hear that, but it's none of my doing. What happened, did your escaped prisoner get back to Germany and give all our secrets away?'

'Sarcasm doesn't suit you.'

164

She flung herself back into the chair and with a shrug he too sat down.

'I met Barbara in the park and we talked about everything. She mentioned that you and Andrew went back a long way and because I was interested in your recovery I asked her about you, but she wouldn't talk about you and that made me feel that they were hiding something about you from me.'

'That's rubbish.'

Isobel leant forward and studied her toes. 'That's what I would have thought except that Alan had already warned me about you.'

There was a long silence. The ticks of the old grandfather clock in the far corner echoed around the room. The kitten that had been fast asleep in the hearth woke up startled as a cinder fell under the grate. Isobel bent down to pick up the kitten and bring it into her lap.

'I see,' Jack said, then getting to his feet he walked out.

'YOU'VE PROVED YOU CAN BE TRUSTED'

Mrs Crombie did not mince her words. 'I was shocked when I heard the gossip, Nurse. For someone in such a responsible position to have her name being bandied about in that disgusting manner is quite unacceptable.'

165

Isobel had invited the magistrate into her home and they stood now face to face on either side of the table. 'Mrs Crombie I have no idea what you have heard, but whatever it is has no bearing on anything I have done or said to bring disgrace to my profession.'

The woman's double chin wobbled with indignation. 'Mr Mackenzie has lodged a complaint against you saying you refused to attend to a dressing on his arm when he asked for help, and that you actually attacked him on one occasion in a public bar. As if that wasn't bad enough we now have people talking about two men fighting over you in that same bar. I know you have just lost your brother nurse but . . .'

'Enough.' Isobel slapped her hand down on the table top.

A stunned Mrs Crombie stood with mouth open and stared at Isobel.

Isobel was the first to recover. 'My apologies, but Mr Mackenzie is a trouble maker as Doctor Turnbull will verify, and as to the fight in *The Apple* I have no idea what it was about.'

'I see. So Mrs Brown was mistaken?'

Isobel gave her visitor a look of confusion before offering her a seat. 'I don't understand what Sylvia has to do with this?'

The magistrate had recovered herself and accepted the chair gratefully. 'I have had some trouble with Mrs Brown's cousin, young

166

Brenda Douglas. So I called around to speak of this matter but Mr Brown was the only person available,' she stopped talking and gave Isobel a knowing look. 'An objectionable man at the best of times,' she said.

Isobel didn't see what any of this had to do with her but waited patiently for the woman to continue.

'He was extremely rude and suggested that I look into more important matters, one being this fight that he said concerned a so-called upstanding member of the community. Not long after which I received Mr Mackenzie's complaint. I was very busy, you understand, with the evacuees. However when I bumped into Mrs Brown on the street she confided in me the details of the upset and what people had been saying about it.'

'Please tell me, Mrs Crombie, because I know nothing of what ensued.'

The woman straightened her shoulders and looked about her. 'There are rumours about you and Captain Lewis and while this is your own business, as long as it is a respectable relationship, that was what the angry exchange was about in the public house. It would appear that the Douglas gal had reported something to Mr Brown and he had foolishly accused the captain of organising, well one can only say improper, parties in the woods.'

Isobel's hand rose to cover her mouth and Mrs Crombie seeing the gesture nodded her head. 'The real reason I am here, Nurse Ross, is because the captain is a close acquaintance of mine and it is important that he be allowed to continue with his work in peace and not be the butt of village gossip.'

'But none of this was my doing,' Isobel protested.

Mrs Crombie's face had taken on a serious demeanour. 'I am aware of that now, my dear, but please in the future be more careful. We cannot take too much care these days.'

Isobel frowned. 'What does Captain Lewis do, Mrs Crombie?'

'Why he looks after the prisoners of war my dear. What else can the poor man do?' With that she rose from her seat indicating that the meeting was over.

After Isobel had seen her out she stood in front of the fire and mulled over all she had learnt. So Jack was afraid for his job. And the mischievous Brenda had repeated to Norman some naughty gossip which had been bad enough to upset Jack to the point of taking a punch at him.

*　　　*　　　*

It was autumn now, the weather had broken and low cloud had once more returned to clothe the hills in mystery. Isobel's breath came in small white puffs as she cycled up the road to Pine Tree Farm.

Jack was never there now when she went to attend to Duncan's vein, which persistently refused to heal.

She propped her bicycle against the wall and called for attention. Today it was the POW who came to shoo away the geese. He was a quiet man with dark eyes and a sober countenance but always courteous. His brows pulled down in a frown as he let her through the gate and waved her towards the kitchen. She turned to see why hc wasn't following her and her heart leapt in her chest as she noted the dark Austin growling up the hill towards the gate. Jack.

In the kitchen her welcome was as warm as it ever was. Today there was an air of suppressed anxiety as Duncan repeatedly urged Bobby to go see if Jack was coming.

'Jack is here now,' she told Duncan.

'Boss won't come until he sees Jack,' Bobby told her when she tried to get them to go into the other room.

'It won't take a minute, Nurse,' Joyce apologised.

'What's all the fuss about?' she asked Joyce.

'The magistrate was up here and took little Brenda Douglas away. The other girl, Margery, is out in the field with Ned, but Dad got himself worked up and nothing would do but that Jack must come.'

When Jack came in through the door Isobel was taking her time washing her hands at the sink.

'What's up now, Dad?' he asked, coming over to where Duncan sat in his chair.

'They've taken the lass away and we need help,' Duncan said.

Jack turned to his mother.

'It's Brenda Douglas, Mrs Crombie came and took her away. She said something about her being in trouble, but your dad's head is full of the news and how the Germans might be invading us and how we have to be on the lookout for spies and he's convinced that Brenda must be a spy.'

Duncan was nodding his head in agreement. Jack bent down and taking his father's hand in his, looked into the other man's anxious face.

'She's working for us, Dad, not the Germans. She's helping the police to find the spies.'

'She's on our side?'

'Yes, Dad.'

'You hear that, Mam, she's on our side.' The lines on his face smoothed out and he smiled. 'Jack says she's on our side.'

And that, Isobel thought, was all it took. If Jack said it was all right then Duncan was happy. Why couldn't it be like that for her, she wondered.

The surgery was crowded that evening and Doctor Turnbull was in a bad mood, so much so that he sent several of his patients off with a flea in their ear. Isobel was kept very busy and

170

it wasn't until the last patient had left and she was tidying up that she noticed how quiet he had gone.

'Is something wrong?' she asked warily expecting a sharp reply snapped back at her.

He looked up from under shaggy brows. 'I need a partner,' he said. 'Someone young that can take night calls; I'm getting too old to be pulled out of bed in the middle of the night.'

Isobel felt her jaw slacken. 'You've always said you would never have a partner getting under your feet.'

'Yes, well, I've changed my mind. There's plenty of room here he can live in.'

'What does Mrs Holland think about that?'

'Nothing to do with the woman.'

'Are you ill?' she asked with concern and a frown pleating her brow.

'No, just tired,' he said rising from his chair.

Isobel's heart skipped a beat, for the first time in the five years she had worked for him, he looked his age. It was in the stiffness when he straightened up and though he wasn't a tall man he appeared shrunken. The wrists that peeped from beneath the leather-edged cuffs of his worn tweed jacket were suddenly thinner than they should have been. He looks so frail, she thought.

Going through into the house she found Mrs Holland in the kitchen. 'The doctor doesn't look too well,' she said, watching the housekeeper preparing the evening meal.

171

'He's just tired,' she said, repeating the doctor's self diagnosis.

Isobel watched the woman work for a while then said, 'I don't think so, I think something is wrong.'

Mrs Holland looked up and smiled across at the worried looking young woman standing on the other side of the table. 'There's a new doctor coming next week to help out for a while.'

'That soon?' Isobel's shocked tone showed her surprise.

'He's a young man who wants to go off and fight, but he has a mild medical condition that means he's unacceptable in the forces.'

Isobel raised her eyebrows in question, and the housekeeper laughed. 'I listened at the door when he came for his interview. Can't be looking after someone if I don't know anything about them now, can I?'

'Did he make a good impression then?'

'Well, you know the doctor. When I asked him he just grunted something and dismissed it. But the young man was the only one who came so I think we can safely say he's the one.'

Oh well here's hoping, she thought, as she left the surgery and headed home, but she still wasn't happy about the doctor and determined to keep an eye on him

* * *

172

Half-past-one in the morning she was woken by repeated knocking on her door. Throwing on her dressing gown and slippers she hurried down stairs. When she opened the door she found a soldier standing on the doorstep.

'Yes, what do you want?'

'There's been an accident up at the camp. Captain Lewis sent me to ask you if you could come with me now, please.'

'You had better come in while I get dressed.' She showed him into the living room then hurried upstairs.

Once ready she followed the soldier down the path to the gate where the usual black car awaited, it was empty. So she climbed into the front seat as the soldier dropped into the driving seat and started the engine.

She tried to engage him in conversation to find out more about what had happened as they headed out to the camp, but he gave little away, then they were turning into the Hall, gates now barricaded and manned. They were stopped by a guard but one look at the soldier driving and they were waved straight through.

Isobel stared at the rows of long huts that sectioned out what had once been parkland to the front of the house. The high wire fence that closed off the woods on one side and the river on the other, while along the bottom the moors rose to cover the high crags and peaks that hide their faces in the clouds.

She was hurried through the main door and

up the grand staircase to a room at the end of the corridor. Here she was met by Jack, while the soldier hurried away.

'Thank you for coming,' Jack nodded and ushered her into the room. A lamp was on by the bed throwing a dull glow across the pale face of Wally stretched out beneath the blankets.

'What's wrong with him?'

'Bullet wound.'

'What?' An astonished Isobel swung round to face him.

'It was an accident.' He was watching her from the scarred side of his face, the shadowed light making the ridged lines and puckered skin appear more damaged than it really was.

She moved over to the side of the bed and Wally gave her a grin. He pushed back the bedclothes and revealed a temporary covering just beneath his shoulder. Smiling back at him she lifted the pad and examined the wound. Replacing it and giving the patient a reassuring smile she turned back to Jack.

'What are you playing at? He should be in hospital. Have you sent for Doctor Turnbull?'

Taking her by the arm he pulled her across to the far side of the room. 'You wanted to know more about me and what I do here? Well I'm going to tell you, but when I do it is on the understanding that you can never, and I mean never, reveal what I am about to tell you to anyone on pain of death, do you understand.'

174

A little annoyed, and if she admitted it, a little afraid even, she stood and stared at him.

He shook her by the arm. 'Do you understand?'

She nodded. 'Yes, yes. I understand.'

'I was ordered up here to create a group of men who would build an underground relay of radio stations to be used in the event of a German invasion. It is on a strictly need-to-know basis and secrecy is top priority. Once in, there is no out.

'Wally was hurt during a practice raid; the other chaps hadn't been warned and returned live fire. We have to deal with his wound here. Anything else would lead to questions being asked. The doctor is not in the know, but it was thought you could be trusted. I hope we don't live to regret it.'

She could feel his stare burning into her, but couldn't lift her face to return it.

'I will need fresh towels and warm water,' she said, reverting back to her professional voice. 'The bullet is still in there.'

Her insides quivered with shock and surprise but outwardly she set about preparing for the coming operation with calm detachment. Firstly she took her bag to one side and went over its contents. Then she asked for and was given alternatives to what she might need. Everything was sterilised in alcohol and the camp first aid box turned over.

The operation was a success. Wally was

resting as Jack rolled down his sleeves and turned towards Isobel with a frown between his brows. 'I hope you realise that what I said earlier wasn't just meant to refer to tonight especially, but for the duration of the war and on if necessary.'

'I heard what you said, and I won't forget,' she said, keeping her back to him. She heard him cross the floor and sensed he was standing close behind her.

'Thank you,' he said quietly.

His breath tickled her neck, her heart raced and she bit down on her lower lip as she put the last objects back into her bag and snapped the clasp.

She turned as though to walk past him but he put out a hand to stop her. 'I'll take you home,' he said.

Her glance never wavered as she said, 'And encourage village gossip? I think not, better someone else takes me.'

His hand dropped to his side as he gave her a brisk nod then left the room.

*   *   *

The next time Isobel saw Sylvia, the pub was closed and Sylvia busy bottling up. She wanted to know what was happening to Brenda.

'I knew she was going to be trouble as soon as she came, but I tried my best with her I really did. Mrs Crombie sent for cousin

Robert, he arrived an hour ago and went straight up to the lodge.'

Isobel tried to comfort her friend. 'I know she's been slacking and flirting, but I think Mrs Crombie has gone over the top this time.'

Sylvia straightened up and wiped a hand across her brow 'I think it's more than that, I think it's something to do with the gossip she spread and Captain Lewis.'

Isobel stood back and stared at her friend. About to spring to Jack's defence she stopped herself and remembered the promise she had made to keep silent.

'The POW at the Lewis's farm,' Sylvia gave a nod of her head. 'Disappeared or was got rid of. You tell me there is nothing going on at that camp.'

At that point Mr Douglas arrived back from the Crombies with Brenda in tow.

'How did it go?' Sylvia called.

'The lass is coming home wi'me.'

Brenda said nothing, but gave them a wink as she followed her dad through to the back. Sylvia shook her head, 'They'll never do anything with her.'

Half-an-hour later as Isobel was on her way out, there was a terrible bang and crash from the back room. The women stared at one another then Sylvia rushed from behind the bar and through the doorway into the house. Isobel heard Sylvia call out and hurriedly followed her. When she entered the room that was the Brown's living room she found Sylvia struggling to lift Norman to his feet.

'What's happened?' she asked hurrying forward to help her friend.

'Cousin Robert punched him.'

'What, who?'

'Brenda's dad. He hit Norman and walked out.'

Norman wore an expression of total incomprehension and Isobel had to smother a guilty grin. If the swollen redness beneath his eye was anything to go by he was going to have a nice shiner to explain away this evening when he opened up.

*   *   *

'Not enough spies around here, Duncan. Brenda has had to go back to Newcastle.' They were doing his exercises and he was still anxious about the Land Army girl.

'Jack said she was one of ours,' Bobby reminded him. 'She should be in the woods with us but she's not. She goes playing in the woods.'

Isobel cast him a sidelong glance, how much does he know, she wondered. For all his slowness he didn't miss much. Had Jack under estimated Bobby? When she left the farm she decided she must phone Jack and arrange to meet him.

Macky was standing alongside the phone

178

box when she returned to the village and because she didn't want him overhearing anything she had to say she headed instead for the post office.

The Misses Simpsons would let her use their phone in an emergency and she felt she wouldn't be telling a lie if that was what she called this.

Jack agreed to call at the cottage that evening and offered to invite the driver to accompany him.

'That won't be necessary,' she said a little stiffly. 'We need to talk privately.'

She thought she sensed humour in his voice when he said, 'Very well then. I'll see you later.'

She sailed through her afternoon cases in a mood that made the pedals on her bicycle sing and such was her good fettle that when Macky turned up at evening surgery she even gave him a smile.

The kettle was on the boil, the best china out, the kitten sleeping in his basket and Phyllis visiting her parents. Isobel had washed and changed out of her uniform, when the knock on the door came. She crossed the floor and opened the door then felt all the colour drain from her face. A man in airforce uniform stood on the doorstep.

'Miss Ross. Miss Isobel Ross?'

Isobel's voice had deserted her so she nodded her head.

'I'm Captain John Philips from RAF Leeming. May I come in?'

She stepped to one side to allow him to enter, then led him through into the living room.

'This is nice,' he said. 'The one thing we all miss, home comforts. My wife does her best, bless her, but her cakes always manage to get demolished before they reach me.'

He has a nice smile, she thought then, but Jack will be here soon.

The airman's face straightened as he said, 'I believe you had notification from the war office about your brother.'

'Yes,'

'Well I have to tell you that we have had some recent information and it would appear that there may be a slim chance that he is still alive. One of our people was picked up by a Norwegian fishing boat but he has yet to be identified.'

His voice and the room came and went with sickening repetition until she convinced herself that she was having some kind of terrible dream, his plane had been seen exploding over the sea after being hit. She was reading the telegram over and over in her head, his death had been witnessed.

Suddenly there was someone else in the room and she didn't have to dream any more, she closed her eyes and sank into the chair.

When she opened them again Jack was

leaning over her with a glass of something in his outstretched hand. 'Take a sip of this, it'll do you good,' he said, pushing the glass towards her.

The glass rattled against the edge of her teeth then the brandy slid down her throat. Coughing she sat forward and pushed the glass away. She glanced around the room then looked up at Jack.

'He's gone.'

Shaking her head she wondered if she had imagined it. She tried to tell Jack what had happened, but found she was afraid in case it wasn't true.

'What did he want?' Jack had replaced the glass on the table and was standing by the fire watching her.

Flapping a hand at him she made to rise from the chair. 'He said there may be a chance that Alan is still alive.' Turning her back on him she made her way to the kitchen.

'They've had word of him?'

'No. Just that a fishing boat picked an Englishman out of the North Sea and they think it might be Alan.'

'Norwegian?'

'Yes.'

She ran the insides of her wrists under the tap and wiped a cold cloth across her forehead. Feeling more human she turned to face Jack who was standing in the living room doorway.

'If it is Alan, the Norwegians will get him home.'

'I know. I hardly dared to hope, it was just the shock.' In the next breath she was asking after Wally. 'When would it be convenient for me to come up and check on him?'

'Wally's fine, you did a good job. His aftercare is nothing our chaps can't handle.'

They returned to the living room and sat down. 'The reason I asked you to come down was because when I was at the farm earlier I spoke to Bobby, or should I say Bobby spoke to me. He was angry because Brenda hadn't been in the woods practising. You had said that she "was one of us", so she should have been in the woods.'

'Umm, that was probably a mistake. Your brother told me that your father taught him to fly, not you?'

'No. I was destined to play around with the wireless, tweaking the cat's whisker and all that.'

'I hoped that might be the case. We need someone to listen in and take messages, could you do that?'

Isobel hesitated, pleating her brows in a frown. Then she was shaking her head slowly from side to side. 'I don't have the time.'

'Not full time of course, just the occasional evening, a couple of hours at the weekend.' He sat forward in his seat elbows resting on his knees. 'The threat of an invasion has died back

182

but there is still much work to be done.'

'But I know nothing of your equipment, we were just playing around.'

'Oh, I'm sure it was a bit more than that, and we have people to show you how to go on. I was wrong to blame you for the gossip, you've proved you can be trusted, now will you do that bit extra for your country and help us out? What would Alan say?'

'You know perfectly well what he would say. It's not that I don't want to help, of course I do, it's just that I feel inadequate to the job.'

'Why don't you come up to the Hall and see for yourself. Meet the other members of the crew. They're a rum bunch, but they all have a skill that is vital to the safety of this country of ours.'

She was hypnotised by a small tic on the good side of his jaw. Secretly she was thrilled to be asked to join in the work of the people at the Hall. To be involved with him in such a serious and dangerous job was more than she had dared wish for. Her eyes travelled up to his. 'Yes, thank you. I would like that.'

He smiled and she saw again that lightening change in his expression.

'Do I call you sir, now?' she asked with a cheeky grin.

'Only on duty.'

*   *   *

183

Walking in the hills not long after learning that Alan may yet be alive, she watched the deer delicately nibbling the last of the leaves from the deciduous trees. She was thinking of his letter to her when they both thought it would be his last and as she breasted the top of the hill there it was, the eagle, a golden flash in the wintry sun.

Shading her eyes she followed his flight as he dipped and soared on the air currents. Nature's mantel was changing, mice, birds and squirrels foraging for food in preparation for the coming winter. Life moved on. Alan would come home and they would continue to fight this war together.

*　　　*　　　*

It was her first night at the Hall. Jack met her at the gates and walked back up the drive with her explaining as he went the procedure she would need to adhere to on future occasions.

'You may meet people you know here but when you leave, you leave that knowledge behind. You are no better acquainted with them tomorrow than you were yesterday. You focus only on the job you do.'

'May I call and see Wally?'

Jack frowned. 'Come back in uniform or as a friend, but not tonight.'

'Right,' she nodded her acceptance.

In the Hall she was handed over to a young

officer who escorted her into the rear of the building to what had probably been the housekeeper's parlour once upon a time, but tonight was a hive of activity.

Her first shock was the sight of Mrs Crombie making her way towards her.

'Nurse Ross, how good of you to join us. Now tonight we only want to see what you know,' she said, bustling her way through the desks and chairs where several men and women sat in front of radios and transmitters and all matter of instrumentation.

She came to a halt in the far corner of the room where a young woman was sitting with earphones on and scribbling away in a note book. 'This is Lisa, she will make you familiar with her equipment. Are you familiar with Morse code?'

'Yes I ...'

'Good then you will pick everything up in no time.' And she marched off back up the room.

Isobel turned to stare at the woman called Lisa who had taken off her earphones and was grinning at her. 'Don't be put off by the dragon,' Lisa laughed, 'she's quite harmless really.'

'Oh I'm not, it's just ...'

'Pull up a chair and we'll get started.'

By the time her three hours were up she was already at her own desk. On her way out she passed a group of officers standing talking in the entrance and with a shock recognised

Andrew Foreman. Why hadn't he seen to Wally's bullet wound, after all he was the doctor, not her.

She put this question to Jack two nights later. 'You were available, Andrew wasn't, it's as simple as that.' She had come up to the Hall to visit Wally who was making a rapid recovery. Jack showed her the way then left her to attend to other work. Wally grinned when he saw her, his only complaint one of stiffness in his arm so she gave him some exercises to do.

'I believe coming to my rescue has caused you some trouble,' he searched her face anxiously.

'Glad to be of help,' she interrupted him. 'Really. It's good to feel useful even if it's in a small way.'

'The captain's pleased to have you with us, he doesn't say much, but what he does say he means and he told me it was good to have you on board.'

'Did he now?'

Wally cocked his head on one side and gave her a considering look. 'He's a hard man to know I'll grant you, and an even harder one to help, but he's been a good friend to me and I'd lay down my life for him. Give him a chance, Nurse, he needs you.'

Isobel was taken aback. 'Strong words, Wally.'

'But true.'

186

The night the bomb dropped above Pine Tree Farm the whole village quaked in excitement. It was their first taste of the real war raging all around them and it was brought home with devastating effect. Shelters that had seen little use to date were suddenly bursting at the seams.

Gas masks that had been carried everywhere but never been outside their boxes except during practice were hauled into life.

Macky Mackenzie and his homeguard stormed the streets bullying the old and infirm who preferred the safety of their own beds come what may, dousing lights that dared to peep from door, torch, or candle. Timmy Green was searching for his dog that had taken fright and run off. While the Simpson sisters had been cooking a late supper and left the gas on.

A baby's cry, a shushed warning to older children as adult ears listened to the sound of an enemy plane in trouble. Men's voices at the doors called along the street. A stuttering then a bang and suddenly the street was full of men running through the allotments, clambering over fences and making a dash to where a small dark figure was floating down from the sky.

Isobel returned to her cottage to find the

187

nose of the plane protruding from the front garden while a large piece of the wing lay on her front step.

'Looks like they've got the Jerry.' It was Constable Burns, indicating a triumphant Macky marching back through the allotments with his prisoner. The man behind him carried the parachute, while others marched protectively around them.

'Are there any injured, Constable?' Isobel asked turning back to the policeman.

'None that I know of, except Timmy Green who fell down in the dark and scraped his knees.'

'I'm sure his mother will manage and I will see him in surgery tomorrow.'

*   *   *

That night Jack was alone in the cockpit. He'd ordered his crew to the back. But couldn't hear himself shout over the drone of the plane. He panicked, he had to get out, but he was strapped securely into his seat. Fighting with demonic strength he hurled Wally across the floor to crash into the wall and lie still.

Suddenly awake he raised his sweat slicked body from the bed to stare in distress at Wally's still form. Throwing himself from the bed, his missing leg forgotten, he lost his balance and fell. Wally came round and holding his head with his good arm squinted

188

stupidly at Jack lying across his legs.

'Captain, Captain, are you all right?'

Jack's shoulders shook with the force of harsh tears. 'Your arm,' he cried, 'I thought . . .'

'No, no harm done, I'll live, come on, Captain, let's get you back to bed.' Both men hauled themselves upward and using Wally's good shoulder as a crutch, Jack manoeuvred himself back onto the bed.

'You're not on duty, man. You're in no fit state,' Jack said, pulling himself together. 'I could have killed you.'

'No sir, not you.'

But Jack wasn't convinced and lay a long time thinking of what might happen some day if he didn't get these nightmares under control. It was all very well taking tablets and being told that it would take time and that eventually his nightmares should get less and less until they faded away altogether. He groaned and turned over.

ISOBEL SPEAKS OF JACK'S DEMONS

That night Isobel couldn't get Wally's words out of her head. When he said that Jack needed her he had sounded so sincere. What, she wondered for the umpteenth time, had made him say that. It was a strange thing for someone so close to him to say.

189

That a man like Jack might need anyone. True she had thought at one time that he might need her friendship if nothing else but he had proved her wrong. He had fought his demons and returned to serve his country once more.

She turned over in her bed and tried to shut out that word, need, but it was virtually impossible for her to do so. She had built her life around other peoples' needs and it was more than she could do to ignore a cry for help.

She would ask Wally what he had meant by those words the next time she saw him she decided next morning as she made herself some breakfast. Nurse Sally Armstrong was helping the doctor at today's surgeries so apart from her daily rounds Isobel was free for the rest of the day.

Pinning her cap to her head she took down the long leather coat she wore in bad weather and picking up her bag left the cottage. Pulling her bicycle from the shed she pushed it down the garden path and was on the point of mounting it when a voice hailed her.

Glancing over her shoulder she saw Barbara Foreman climbing down from a small Ford car. Turning the bike around she walked towards the car. Barbara waved to her and as she drew closer she could see that the car was full of children. Looking flushed but happy Barbara cried, 'I'm glad I caught you, I need to ask you a favour.'

There's that word again, she thought. 'I was about to go out on my rounds, but how can I help?'

'Do you recognise them?' she asked turning back to the car.

Isobel glanced at the children peering out of the car windows. 'Should I?'

Barbara laughed. 'There are five of them.'

'I can see that, whose are they?'

'Ours, Andrew's and mine.'

Isobel stared at her with a lift of her eyebrows. And Barbara went on to explain. 'The two girls are our original evacuees, then there are the three Heron children Mrs Crombie talked us into taking, and my life has never been so full. But what I was wanting to ask you is a real favour, can you possibly babysit for me on Thursday afternoon? Andrew is so busy these days and I have an important appointment that I really should not miss. I know you will probably be working but I thought there might just be a chance.'

Isobel thought carefully then said, 'Well I have my rounds in the morning and I'm doing morning and evening surgery but I have a couple of hours in the afternoon if that will do.'

'Oh that will be wonderful, thank you so much,' and before Isobel could say any more Barbara was back in the car and calling a cheery 'goodbye.'

Shaking her head, Isobel mounted her bicycle and set off. She had never had much to do with young children other than to attend to sick ones and had no idea how on earth she was going to cope with caring for five of them for an afternoon.

*　　　*　　　*

Wednesday morning found her back at the Hall visiting Wally, who was allowed to do light work while he waited for his shoulder to heal. That morning he was alone at a desk leafing through some paperwork. 'Hello, Nurse,' he greeted her.

After passing the time of day and asking after his health she leant towards the desk from her seat and asked quietly, 'What did you mean when you said that Jack needed me?'

Wally didn't look up, simply fluttered more pages of paper. 'I shouldn't have said anything, Miss. It's none of my business.'

'Please Wally, you can't wriggle out of it now. What did you mean, is Jack in trouble?'

He was looking decidedly uncomfortable now. He grabbed up a sheaf of papers and stood up to leave. 'I have to get these over to the other office, so if you will excuse me, Miss.'

'No, Wally. I mean to get an answer if I have to go to Jack myself.'

'The captain is fine really.'

'Does he know you go around telling people

he needs them?'

The papers came back down onto the desk as he slumped back into his chair. 'He doesn't get much sleep and I worry that he is pushing himself too hard.'

'Well surely as a pilot he was used to going without sleep.'

'For short spells, yes, but he never gets a night's rest. The doctor gives him pills but,' and he shook his head.

Isobel was frowning 'Do you mean when you say he never gets a night's rest that he has nightmares, but that's only to be expected after his terrible ordeal, surely?'

Wally looked around anxiously as though searching for a way out. 'Yes, that's what the doctors say and that in time they will fade. In the meantime they are driving the poor man mad. He won't accept it you see, none of it.'

Puzzled now, Isobel said, 'But I thought when he left hospital and went down south, well he was so much better when he came back.'

Shaking his head Wally said, 'Only because he hides it. He won't talk about it to anyone. Doctor Foreman and the captain go back a long way, but I don't believe he has ever spoken to him other than to ask him for more tablets. I know the doctor doesn't like to give him so many pills, but . . .' and here he shrugged helplessly. 'He can't let him suffer.'

Once more Isobel was hearing Alan's

Isobel couldn't help but smile at Barbara's sudden transformation into instant motherhood of this large family.

So sidetracked was she that she didn't notice Jack come up alongside her until he asked, 'Can I give you a lift back to Thornbury?'

Barbara had disappeared towards the kitchen with Andrew trailing after her.

'Yes, thank you. I came on the bus but I would be glad of a lift back if that is convenient.'

'No problem,' he said, then called down the passage to say they were leaving.

Barbara appeared around the kitchen door. 'Oh right, well thanks for everything Isobel, you really are a brick. I don't know what I would have done if you hadn't stepped into the breach.'

As they hurried out to the car Jack said, 'Helping out again? Is there no end to your willingness to find people in need.'

She opened her mouth to say something as they climbed into the car but it was a strange driver this time and she bit her tongue, better to wait until they were alone.

Arriving back in the village she turned to Jack and asked him if he could come down to the cottage one evening soon.

With a questioning look he asked, 'Is it urgent?'

His question caught her by surprise, and

196

much to her disgust she found herself floundering. 'Well no, not exactly, but, there was something I wanted to ask you about.'

'What about the girl?'

'She's back at the vicarage with her parents now the Heron children are with Barbara.'

'Is it personal?'

She gave him a hard look. He hadn't left the car to walk her to her door as he had always done in the past and their relationship felt suddenly frail and unfamiliar. Taking a deep breath she said, 'Yes, it is actually.'

Then it was his turn to be taken unaware and with a smile twisting his lips he said, 'Then of course I will make every effort to be down tomorrow evening.'

'After surgery,' she said, turning away and stomping off down the path.

'Naturally,' she heard him say as the car drove off.

*   *   *   *

When she arrived back from surgery the next night Jack was waiting on the doorstep.

'You should have gone straight in, the door's never locked.'

'Well it should be! Don't you ever learn, woman? What if that soldier had come back and let himself in?'

Isobel shuddered. 'No-one locks their doors around here.'

'Times are changing. There are more strangers around these days.'

'I suppose so,' she said, preceding him into the cottage. She hung up her leather coat and tugged off her cap then set about making a warming cup of cocoa as her tea ration was nearly finished.

Jack had crossed into the living room and commandeered the old chair and was playing with the kitten. Isobel stood silently in the doorway and watched him as she waited for the milk to boil.

Instinct told him he was being watched and he asked, 'Well, what is that we have to discuss that is so personal?'

The milk boiled and she made their drinks. Carrying the two mugs she came into the front room and handed one to him before settling herself down in the chair opposite.

'Well?' he said, looking at her expectantly.

She cradled the hot mug in her hands and toyed with how she might start. 'I was thinking about Alan. Wondering how he might cope with what he has been through should he still be alive. They said his plane exploded, he may have been badly hurt when they brought him out of the water. I want to know what I may be up against when he comes home. You are the only person that can help me.'

There followed a long silence, then he asked in a voice full of weary anger, 'Who put you up to this?'

She didn't bother to deny that he was the real problem. 'Someone who is very worried about you.'

'There is only one person who can know and he would never . . .' He stopped himself. 'He has been sworn to secrecy.'

'So have I, but that does not preclude him from personal information if it concerns the wellbeing of the officer in charge.'

'Is he saying I am failing in my duty?' His voice was soft but each word came out with the strike of a stone.

I have to put a stop to this, she thought desperately. Go back to the beginning and start again. Her heart was jumping madly in her chest as she licked her lips and prepared to try again. 'It was Wally. He told me you were not sleeping. I asked him if he wanted me to have a word with Doctor Turnbull but he said Andrew Foreman was treating you. He asked me if I would speak to you.'

He had risen from the chair and wandered over to the old piano in the far corner of the room. The tension between them was so heavy she felt afraid to breathe. The kitten had curled up in the warmth of his empty seat. He lifted the lid of the piano and brushed his fingers over the yellowed keys.

'Do you play?' he asked.

'No, Alan does.'

'I have nightmares,' he said dropping the lid and coming back to the hearth. 'That is why I

199

can't sleep. The same nightmare every night with slight variations. Sometimes I am violent. Wally is good at explaining away the odd bruise or black eye.

'I have tablets, they don't stop the nightmares or help me sleep but they do stop the screaming.' He was leaning back against the mantel and staring at the floor, as though disapproving of some speck of dust he had seen.

'And the hospital tells you they will fade in time.'

'Yes.'

'But you need that sleep now.'

'Yes.'

'When I was a little girl I would snuggle up on my father's knee and he would tell me stories of his war. One of those stories was of a friend of his who had come back shell-shocked and in a bad way. The family were having a hard time with him until a grandmother put the youngest child in the bed with him. He slept soundly thereafter.'

He was staring at her his dark eyes shining like wet coals in the overhead light.

Then he let out such a laugh, full of bitter pain that Isobel jumped in her seat. 'And where do you suggest I get this child from, grab the next one I see from its pram outside a shop, or perhaps Barbara would lend me one of hers. How should I frame my explanation, what could I say that won't be misinterpreted, let me see . . .'

Isobel took a big gulp of air. Even the good side of his face was twisted with misery, and before she could stop herself she had blurted out. 'I will settle with you. I'll sit by your bed and hold your hand.'

An ember fell into the grate leaving a rustle of settling coals. The kitten woke, stretching and yawning, then looked around for something to play with.

Isobel hunted desperately for her professional self. 'For comfort only, you understand, as people in the open do for bodily warmth. Once you are asleep I shall go.'

The laughter had gone from his face, when with slumped shoulders he gently moved the kitten from the chair and sat down.

'Always the caring nurse, still trying to mend everyone's problems.' He reached across the gap to take her hands in his. 'You must know you can't cure them all and yet you never give up trying, do you?'

Silent now, Isobel's glance never left her hands.

He stood up and slowly pulled her to her feet. Then placing his hands on either side of her head he stooped to lay his mouth on hers. His mouth was cool and firm as he laid it on her warm soft lips. The kiss was light and brief; when she sensed his withdrawal she kissed him back. There was a moment of hesitancy then they were in each other's arms all else forgotten.

201

'I THOUGHT I'D LOST YOU'

Alan was safe and recovering from his ordeal at a convalescence hospital outside of Malton. As soon as she received the letter she had cleared her workload with Doctor Turnbull and arranged to travel down to see the brother she had feared she would never see again.

She couldn't help but wonder how he would react when she told him about Jack and how close they had grown. She smiled to herself when she remembered how Alan had warned her that Jack was deep and secretive, but that didn't matter now as she was sure he would understand when she had explained.

Jack had been a frequent visitor to the cottage since the night he had revealed his terror of the nightmares he suffered. They had talked often and gradually Jack had learnt to relax in her company. Some nights now he managed to get a whole night's sleep without a nightmare.

That night she was due to finish her training up at the Hall after which she would be on stand by, ready to help out should she be needed. She would tell Jack then of the letter about Alan and how she was to go down to visit him. She knew he would be pleased for her.

She finished her rounds early, arranged for

her neighbour to look after the kitten, ate her tea, pumped up yet another flat tyre and set off for the Hall. When she arrived she propped her bicycle against the wall and hurried up the steps to the main entrance. Jack was nowhere to be found when she bumped into Wally.

'Have you seen Jack?' she asked breathlessly.

'He's out on ops.'

'Oh dash, I wanted to see him before I left. Will you let him know my brother is home and in hospital in Malton. I'm off down to see him and I should be home the day after tomorrow.'

'Righty-oh, Miss and I'm right glad to hear about your brother.'

'Thank you, Wally. Now I must dash before Mrs Crombie crosses me off.'

*　　　*　　　*

The journey to Malton the following day was arduous with crowded platforms and busy trains. Even the corridors were packed with soldiers sitting on kit bags. She had to change trains twice in a desperate scramble, once when she nearly lost her case and again when a lost child attached himself to her and she had to spend time finding his parents. But eventually she arrived at her destination.

It was the same old Alan she found sitting up in bed grinning at her and she sighed with relief. Rushing over to him she flung her arms around his neck threatening to throttle him.

'Hold on, girl. You're choking me!'

She sat back and looked lovingly at him, feeling herself choking up inside. The man in the next bed made some comment that made Alan chuckle. 'No such luck. The girl's my sister.'

'Are you all right, no injuries?'

'Nothing that won't heal.'

She held his hand and he squeezed hers. 'I thought I'd lost you.'

'Sorry.'

They stared into each other's eyes then with a slight shrug Isobel said, 'I brought you some homemade toffee.'

She took a taxi into town and stayed in a B&B overnight. The following day she visited him again. This time she told him about Jack, how he had opened up to her and how they were now good friends.

'Friends?' he asked with a frown between his brows.

'I'm very fond of him, Alan, and I hope you and he will be friends too.'

His face split in a smile. 'Any friend of yours will be good enough for me.'

'Good,' she said bending forward to place a kiss on his cheek. 'I have to go back tonight, but I'll see you soon.'

He nodded. 'I have two more weeks here then a spot of leave.'

She walked away down the ward turning at

the entrance to wave to him, and then hurried to the station to catch the train home. There was a group of soldiers playing cards in her carriage and a businessman reading a newspaper opposite.

This train only necessitated one change-over for which she was profoundly grateful. That was until it pulled into a siding in Northallerton. No-one took any notice for a while. Then the elderly gentleman opposite folded his paper and looked around. The soldiers' card game came to an end and they, too, started to take an interest in their surroundings. The men in the corridors were climbing over luggage and kit bags to gather at the door and hang out of the window.

The soldiers in the carriage forced open their door and called along to ask what the hold-up was. When he received only a garbled reply he withdrew his head and answered the businessman's query with a shrug of his shoulders. More time passed and it was growing dark. Isobel worried that she would miss her train in Newcastle.

Two-and-a-half hours later they felt a bumping and jarring and it was rumoured that they had exchanged trains and were now about to continue their journey. She had missed her connection by three-quarters-of-an-hour when she arrived in Newcastle. What was worse, it had been the last train. She stood on the platform as others milled around her wondering what on earth she was going to do now.

As she headed for the bus station she knew it would take three buses to get her back to Thornbury, but at this time of the evening the chances that all three would be running was doubtful.

Leaving the train station she was about to cross the road when a large black Austin pulled up in front of her. The door was flung open and a familiar voice called for her to get in.

'How did you know?' she asked climbing in beside Jack.

'We pick up all kinds of messages in our job.' He grinned. 'How did you find Alan?'

She turned to him eagerly and told him all about her visit.

Back in the cottage they fell into each other's arms until Jack murmured close to her ear. 'I can't keep Wally waiting.'

*   *   *

Back on her rounds the following day she bumped into Meg Foster who despite everything had given birth to a healthy baby boy and was looking much fitter.

'Are you still at Beacon Hill?' Isobel asked her.

'No, Nurse. They wanted my cottage for one of their lads. But we're to be fine, me and the kids. I've been visiting Mr Heron, and he's so much better now and looking forward to leaving the hospital. He's bought himself a house out Dumfries way and wants me and the kiddies to go with him and take care of things.'

'My goodness. You'll have your hands full with his three and your own four children to look after.'

'Oh, they'll be no problem, but I told him I have no learning for housekeeping. But he up and told me it wasn't important, only that I was a good worker and had a kind heart. So I reckon I'm onto a good thing.'

Isobel smiled. 'I think you very well might be at that, Meg. Good luck to you and the children.'

*　　　*　　　*

The new doctor had arrived when Isobel reported for evening surgery that night. Michael Heeligan was his name. Doctor Turnbull introduced him with a scowl.

After the new doctor had retreated into the house and Isobel was on the point of ushering in their first patient, Doctor Turnbull growled, 'I suppose now we will be pulled out with all the women in the village developing minor ailments.'

Isobel smothered a smile. It was true that Doctor Heeligan was quite the handsomest man to have been seen in these parts for some time. And true to word, the following surgeries were so busy the patients were queuing out of the door.

Another room had been opened up at the rear of the house for Doctor Heeligan and in no time at all the patients were swapping seats in the waiting room for the chance to be seen by the new doctor.

Doctor Tumbull's temper did not improve with the easing of his work load and Isobel became more convinced than ever that there really was something wrong with him. Again she questioned Mrs Holland as to what could be the matter. The housekeeper frowned and agreed that something must be done.

'He won't take any notice of me, but perhaps if you were to speak to him?'

'He would chew me up.'

The housekeeper nodded. 'But you might find out what is wrong with him first.' The two women looked at one another sizing up a difficult situation then Isobel sighed. 'I suppose,' she said.

She chose her moment carefully two nights later when the last patient had just left after being told there was nothing wrong with them that a tot of whisky and lemonade wouldn't put right.

'Now Doctor Heeligan is here, why don't you go to visit your daughter in Edinburgh?'

He was rifling through a drawer looking for something he had mislaid when Isobel spoke.

He looked up. 'And why would I want to do that? I haven't seen the woman for ten years.'

'Well you have never had the time before. Now you have.'

'What's that woman been complaining about now?' he snapped, slamming the drawer shut. 'Have you seen that paper? I left it here on my desk.'

'Mrs Holland hasn't been complaining about anything. We just thought you might need a change now that Doctor Heeligan is here to take the workload.'

'She's been in here again and moved that paper.' He was scrabbling through a cupboard behind his desk. 'I've told the woman until I'm sick, not to touch my papers.'

Isobel sighed. 'Is this it,' she asked, picking up a file of loose papers and offering it to him. He snatched it from her hand and tucking it under his arm left the room. Isobel's frown deepened. Now she was really worried.

*   *   *

Michael Heeligan took the next two surgeries and when Isobel enquired after Doctor Turnbull she was told that he had gone to his daughter's in Edinburgh. Mrs Holland confirmed this when Isobel called into the kitchen after work.

'He made his mind up on the spur of the moment. You know what he's like. It was the

209

new doctor that persuaded him finally. Clever young man he is and no bother to look after. It's a pleasure to cook for him, not like Albert who grouses at everything.'

'Albert?' Isobel gasped. 'Doctor Turnbull's name is Albert?'

'Yes, didn't you know? Albert Joseph Reynolds Turnbull. That's what it says on his birth certificate. I had to collect it for him on one occasion, it was open and I saw it.'

'How long is he away for?'

'He didn't say. Perhaps Doctor Heeligan knows.'

She wasn't due on duty until Wednesday morning so the first thing she did when she arrived at the surgery was to speak to Doctor Heeligan.

'Do you know when Doctor Turnbull is returning?'

'I'm afraid not. I wonder if you would be so kind as to show our new receptionist around.'

'Receptionist?'

'Well you must admit we need one, with two rooms busy you are run off your feet trying to cover both.'

*   *   *

Things were changing Isobel admitted to herself as she did her rounds that afternoon. What on earth would Doctor Turnbull say when he came home and found a receptionist installed in the little cloakroom at the back door.

Michael Heeligan might be good looking but his character left a lot to be desired. He behaved as though he had been given *carte blanche* to do whatever he wanted to the surgery and Isobel knew Doctor Turnbull would never have agreed to that.

She was concentrating on finding a new address that she hadn't visited before when she realised that the person on her list was in fact one of Nurse Thompson's patients.

She tackled Michael Heeligan about this error when she returned to the surgery and was told that from now on the two nurses would divide the calls between them.

'But that won't work. The patients get used to one particular nurse seeing them each time.' As she spoke she thought of what Duncan would have to say if Nurse Thompson and she called on alternate visits. 'Our patients get used to us.'

'I'll grant you that, Nurse, but on the other hand it will give you more time in the surgery so we can set up special clinics for the children and the old.'

'What does Doctor Turnbull have to say about all this?'

She could feel her temper rising. Who did this upstart think he was? People thought the world of Doctor Turnbull and the practice had worked perfectly well for years suiting all patients.

'I have bought the practice from Doctor Turnbull and he won't be returning, I'm afraid.'

This statement hit Isobel like a hammer blow. 'Won't be returning?' she whispered. 'Why ever not?'

'Doctor Turnbull is ill, Nurse Ross. His daughter, as I'm sure you are aware, is a nursing sister at the Royal in Edinburgh. When he knew there was no cure for his illness he made the brave decision to go to the hospital so that the doctors there could carry out tests on him to try to discover more about the illness. He didn't want a fuss so said goodbye to no-one. Please don't feel hurt by his neglect. It was, I am sure, to save you becoming upset as much as himself. I hope you will serve me as well as you did him, it is after all the same practice.'

'I will have to think about that, Doctor. I realise things will change but I am not sure that I am prepared to change with them. Good day.'

*　　　*　　　*

Two weeks later Alan came home on leave. She had promised to take him up to Pine Tree Farm to meet the Lewises, but before she did that she wanted to talk to him about Jack and their future.

212

When Jack appeared late one afternoon she had to leave them together to go to evening surgery. She worried and fretted all through surgery wondering what was happening and couldn't wait to get home again, only to find the cottage in darkness.

On the point of going up to *The Apple* herself she stopped and took a deep breath. They would come back eventually and whatever they had decided about the other they wouldn't be telling her, so she might as well stop fussing, she scolded herself.

She was in bed when she heard them return. There was the odd bang and shushing, giggles and hushed words. Well, she thought, they are both here and it doesn't sound as though they have fallen out. She heard the tap in the kitchen then footsteps coming upstairs. She held her breath, there were two sets of footsteps surely, she sat bolt upright in bed.

They turned into the back bedroom with its old double bed. The bedsprings groaned, low voices could be heard through the wall then nothing. Isobel tossed and turned all night but apart from the sound of snoring there was no more noise from next door.

Next morning she was up making porridge in the kitchen when Alan arrived behind her to ask what was to eat. He looked tired.

'Did you have a good night?'
'Sorry we were a bit late.'
'We?'

213